I0680452

Neeta Lyffe, Zombie Exterminator in

Shambling in a
Winter Wonderland

Karina Fabian

LASER COW
PRESS

Laser Cow Press

MERRITT ISLAND, FL

Laser Cow Press
Merritt Island, FL
https://fabianspace.com

Book Layout © 2017 BookDesignTemplates.com
Cover art by Karina Fabian

I Left My Brains in San Francisco/ Karina Fabian. – 2nd ed.
ISBN 978-1-956489-06-4

*For every military member who's ever deployed.
We salute you and thank you for your sacrifice,
dedication, and hard work.*

Napalm sticks to Zombies!

Contents

Chapter 1

Neeta's mother had told her the only time she should run with scissors was when a zombie was involved. Neeta wondered what her mother would have said about surfing with a katana.

"Ted, this is our stupidest idea ever," she said through teeth that chattered with a combination of cold, adrenalin, and fear.

Even so, no one would notice from the way she stood staring out at the surf, clad in a head-to-toe wetsuit and a motorcycle helmet bearing the logo of her business, Lyffe-Undeath Exterminations. The utility belt at her hip held the tools of her trade—this time, napalm grenades. Expensive stuff, but the cheaper products would get washed away by the ocean before they had a chance to work. She'd used some straps from the emergency kit in her van to tie on the sheath for the katana, which was borrowed for the job. Her monofilament sword would not work in the water. She braced her surfboard in one hand and steadied the pommel of the newly sharpened sword in the other. She dug her toes into the sand to release her nervousness.

Before her, the late-winter waves of Redondo Beach surged and retreated, uncaring of her discomfort or of the zombie hanging ten on its crests. For the past three days, she and Ted had been taking shifts with three other teams of exterminators waiting for the lamebrain to get bored and come to shore to seek a snack or build a sandcastle or do anything on dry land so they could behead it. But whoever the rotter had been in life, he had been intense about surfing. Finally, this morning, they had all met to decide on a new plan of action.

Somehow, that plan ended with her and Ted "volunteering" to surf out to the zombie and take it out in its own element.

When had her life gotten so strange? She'd been a zombie exterminator for years, and until recently, she'd encountered them in backyards and alleyways, the occasional restaurant or warehouse. Just her, her chainsaw, and the cleaning products that repelled zombies. Dangerous, sure, but ordinary. Yet in the last two years, she'd taken on not just singles but entire hordes in traffic jams, coming out of underwater graves, in the sickest refinery she'd ever seen…and now on a surfboard.

Was it because of her time on Zombie Death Extreme? Had her brush with Hollywood fame brought all the karmic craziness out looking for her? Or was it just something about the 2040s?

"This is insane," she said. "Our dumbest stunt yet."

"I know, babe," Ted, her fiancé and business partner said, though he didn't sound nearly as nervous as she felt. Not that he would. He was an adrenalin junkie with a taste for the bizarre.

Maybe he's the reason my life has taken such a wild turn. She smiled at the thought. If so, that was fine by her. All the insanity of her recent life was worth it for bringing him to her.

He was clad in a similar outfit, and despite the cold beach and the job before them, Neeta couldn't help but notice how good he looked in it.

They had to set a wedding date soon or she'd go crazy with waiting. He also had a katana, its point jammed into to the wet sand. His cousin would be furious. She'd lent them the weapons with the promise they'd be careful with them. She had a thing for authentic—and sharp—swords.

Ted scanned the horizon with a small pair of binoculars. The first evening, snuggled under blankets with the surf illuminated by the ocean, had been so romantic. The fact that they'd been wearing hazmat suits and watching an undead surfer through night vision binoculars, aware that at any moment they might have to doff their cozy nest and give chase with swords blazing, had only heightened the experience.

Once again, she had to admit to herself that she had a twisted sense of romance.

Not that Ted had complained. He got into the mix of danger and romance more than the latest incarnation of James Bond. Yet even he seemed a little hesitant about jumping into the winter ocean after a surfing zombie.

"We're nuts, the both of us," she said, not sure if she was talking about the job or their relationship. Not that she wanted to give up on either.

Ted shrugged philosophically. "I know, but it's not like we can do much about it. It's a protected beach. No boats."

"It's ridiculous. We just need a rowboat, even."

"'Oars are an act of aggression against jellyfish and other peaceful aquatic creatures.'" He quoted the pamphlet they'd been required to read and acknowledge before being allowed on the beach. "Remember the uproar when that kayaker knocked out Dilly the Dolphin? We're lucky to get to use the boards. That corpsicle has been out there for four days. Even my cousin Huu doesn't love surfing that much."

"Kind of gives support to the theory that the zombie desire for brains is culturally inbred, doesn't it?"

Zombies, while mindless, retained certain habits and attitudes they'd held in real life. Usually, this made their job easier, as they could use that knowledge to trap them. This time, however, she'd give anything to be able to confront a mindless Romero zombie shambling menacingly and demanding her brains.

"Yeah. Too bad the hamburger trick didn't work. Everyone's tired of patrolling without getting paid, our client is getting impatient, and we have a vacation to get ready for."

"It's a publicity thing," she retorted automatically, "for the van." Three more years doing publicity for HumVans, and it was hers, free and clear. She didn't like using her reputation for someone else's advertising, but it was the only way she'd ever afford a tricked-out exterminator's ride.

"So? You don't have to pose in front of the van all week. Even better, Utah is a zombie-free state. We are going to have so much fun—once we take out the Undead Shredder. There he is! Looks like he's just lying on his board, taking in the sun."

He passed her the binoculars. As she scanned where he pointed, the waves picked up just enough to give her a good angle. Their target must have died recently; although the skin had that bloated, waterlogged look of someone who'd been in the water way too long, the zombie was still intact. They'd checked with the authorities, but no one had reported a missing male that matched its description. Probably some single guy on vacation, died who-knew how, and came back determined to make the most of his holiday, anyway.

Regardless, she was glad to see the tanned skin and relatively few signs of decay. After dealing with the squishy undead on the beach at San Francisco the past summer, she had seen enough waterlogged zombies to last her a lifetime.

It lay flat on its back, its arms crossed. Coffining. Did it have enough brain power to understand irony?

At least it didn't look like Bergie. She had finally banished the nightmares of Donald Eidleberg surfing beside her, holding the head she severed from his shoulders. She did not want to encounter anything like that in real life.

"Why couldn't it come back to shore to relax?" she complained as she handed back the glasses for him to tuck into a pocket of his belt.

"Waiting for the next big wave. Besides, it's peaceful out there. You know, just you, the ocean beneath your board, the sun warm on your face."

"Not in January." It was calm at the moment, but over the past few days, they'd seen waves taller than her house. More than once, their quarry had shot out of the tube like a bat out of hell.

"In our favor. It won't get spooked by our wetsuits." He turned from the ocean to give her an appreciative look. "And may I just say that you look incredibly hot, Future Mrs. Lyffe-Hacker? We have got to set a wedding date."

There were times when she could not bear to be still under that gorgeous scrutiny.

Mind on the job, Lyffe. Focus. They were there to do a job. Besides, kissing was awkward in the helmets, despite the wide visor area.

"That's on the vacation to-do list," she replied briskly. "Come on, let's get out there. Maybe we can decapitate it before the waves pick up again. Whoever it was in life was a fuze core surfer."

Ted retrieved his sword and sheathed it. He had an actual belt for it from his cousin. "Maybe, but we're no slouches, and we're motivated. Let's shred the waves and the rotter. Cowabunga!"

They lowered the visors on their helmets, grabbed their boards, and raced to the surf. Ted shouting, "Vacation!" as he ran.

Neeta swore as they hit the water. "I hate the cold!" she complained to Ted over the mic in her helmet.

At least the helmet was waterproof. It had been specially designed to protect the face from zombie spoor in case an extermination got messy—and it seemed Neeta's fate to deal with messy exterminations. Her arms sliced through the water, occasionally bumping the sheath that flopped at her side. She should have tied it to her leg. Despite the wetsuit, the cold seeped into her muscles, making them harder to work. She vowed never to give up her regular chainsaw workouts. The monofilament swords might be more efficient, but there was nothing like the heft of a Decapitator 4000 for building upper body strength.

A small swell approached, and they duckdived under it, careful to angle their heads so the water didn't invade their helmets. Their zombie target wouldn't be interested in some little whitewater. It was further out, waiting for a big swell. Their customer, the beach caretaker, had called in when he'd seen it riding the pipeline. He'd thought it was some crazy, fish-hating hotdogger from up North until it wiped out and surfaced missing part of its arm.

Further from shore, the chop got heavier. The waves were picking up. Neeta gritted her teeth and forced her arms to work harder, but all too soon, she felt her muscles burn from the effort. Neeta was panting when Ted paddled up beside her and jerked his head to the left.

"There he is." he panted.

She followed his example and sat up on her board, legs dangling in the water, although her slippered feet were already freezing.

"How you want to do this?" she asked.

"Ride a swell over and wipe out beside him? I can chop him as I fall."

"Please tell me you're joking!"

He laughed. "Easy, Boss. I'm not sure even I'm that good. Napalm grenades? Little Greek fire on the waves?"

That sounded enticingly warm. "Now you're talking! Let's hurry. The surf is picking up."

"Too late!"

Ted pointed at a rising swell. It was bodacious—or would have been on a summer day with a beach full of living people out to catch some hot rays and cool waves. Their zombie had sensed it and had spun around to catch it. With part of its arm missing, it paddled at an angle away from Neeta and Ted. The only hope for catching it now was to surf high and hope to use the power of the wave for speed.

Neeta swore—in Hawaiian; it seemed appropriate—and paddled furiously toward the growing wave. It promised to be ten feet at least. She was so glad Ted had been pushing her this summer. Who'd have thought she'd use her skills on a board in her job?

"Another wave coming. Take this one," Ted told her. He duckdived under.

"Our life is weird!" she shouted to Ted as she caught the wave, popped up, and serpentined across the top, staying ahead of the pocket. She was not up to shacking, not with a 12-foot tube of ice-cold water. The surf socks Min had given her for Christmas worked like a charm, making it easy to grip the board as she shifted her weight heel and toe. Her "fish" responded beautifully, tracing a clean and, more importantly, speedy path toward where she'd last seen the zombie. The helmet's oversized visor allowed for a 180-degree field of vision, but she still had a hard time maneuvering and keeping it in her sights.

There! It was still on its belly, heading for the next wave. She reached for a grenade as she shot past it.

A small rise took her by surprise, and she lost her balance. She hit the water hard, head back, chin tilted. At that angle, nothing kept water from seeping in under her helmet. The waterlogged weight of it dragged her down as she fought against panic and to hold what little breath she had. The current pulled at her. From a reef below her, angry Garibaldi fish shot from their hiding places in her direction.

She flailed then kicked hard, propelling herself to the surface. Fortunately, the leash had worked, and her board floated nearby. She struggled onto its reassuring surface. She raised the visor and water spilled out. She spat to expel the saltwater in her mouth and gasped in air until she had enough breath to swear.

"Babe, where are you? I've got our rotter in sight. We're coming your way. Ready? Babe?"

Neeta could barely hear him for the rush in her ears and the sound of her coughing. She sat on the board, gripping the rails. She'd lost her grenade.

The wave lifted her and she tensed her legs to keep her seat as years of lessons and practice took over, and she paddled a bit further sideways to where the wave looked like it would calm. She turned the board toward the breaking swell. She was not drowning without taking out their corpsicle first!

There it was, cool as could be, riding the pocket, caressing the wave with its stump of an arm. She didn't see Ted. Was he going to shoot the tube, or had he wiped out, too?

She tightened her legs around the fat board and drew the katana. If she had to, she'd paddle over the crest and take it out at the knees on her way down the wave.

"Vacation!" Ted hollered as he sped between her and the zombie. With the power of the wave propelling him, he moved almost too quickly for her to react. Even so, he lobbed the grenade, pinwheeling his arms as he nearly lost his balance.

The grenade splattered against the zombie. The jellied gasoline spread and engulfed the undead in flames. She cheered and raised the sword.

The wave crested before her, and she let it pull her backward.

With a sudden wash of spray and flame, the zombie arched off the wave right over her.

Neeta took in a huge gasp of air that was as much in surprise as intentional, grabbed her board and Eskimo rolled just as it skipped past her. She heard splats as bits of napalm-enflamed zombie splattered on the bottom of her board. She kicked hard with the current to push away before rolling upright. She raised her visor, took in a huge breath and swore through chattering teeth. Somehow, she'd kept hold of the sword.

She felt warmth to her right and turned to see the zombie lying flat on its board beside her. Over the pounding of the waves and the roaring of the flames, she could hear it moan, "Wahine."

Shrieking with disgust, she swung down and took out the zombie at the neck. Her board tilted toward it, and she released the sword to counter-balance before she tumbled off. She kicked the zombie's board to push the corpse away from her.

The next wave came, gentler this time, but she lay flat on the board and rode the wave on her stomach. She'd had enough surfing for one day.

Once the water had calmed again, she sat on the board, gripping her rails, coughing and blinking water from her eyes. Her arms and legs ached. Her eyes and nose burned from the salt water. The whole encounter had taken maybe 10 seconds, but she felt like she'd been working for hours. She didn't see their rotter anywhere.

"Ted, where are you? Do you see it? Ted?"

Great. The comms were out. Probably full of seawater. They'd just bought this helmet over the summer. Did the lifetime warranty cover rekills in the open sea? Full submersion on an official extermination?

Her life was so bizarre.

Ted paddled up to her and tapped her shoulder. He pointed to the right, where the surfboard and zombie floated, flaming like a Viking funeral pyre. "Good job, Boss."

"I don't think I got the head clean off."

Sitting calm and composed, as if he always went hunting undead on surfboards, Ted pulled out his binoculars. "Nope. Looks like it's on an angle and partly wedged into the board. I think you got the spine, though."

"That is a sharp katana! Remind me to compliment your cousin." He handed her the binoculars, but she shook her head. Water sloshed around her ears.

"Hope the helmet cam caught it all. Judi's going to go crazy bragging to her friends how her sword took out an actual zombie. Isn't it cute, though? We should call it Bob."

"I just want to call it Rekilled. Let's get it to shore so we can get paid and go get ready for our vacation. Utah may be cold, but at least it's dry, right?" She pulled off her helmet and shook it out. A confused jellyfish splatted onto the board.

She smacked it off. "Lucky I didn't get stung."

"Just hope it doesn't file a complaint." Ted snickered, and she couldn't stop herself from giggling, too. They laughed until the next wave came to take them and their rekill to shore.

Her life in California might be weird, but maybe in Utah, she could relax with an ordinary vacation.

Chapter 2

Olivia Darnell eased her snowmobile to a gentle stop several yards from the snow pit. Rebar held up a line of blue barrier tape bearing the message: "USWS INVESTIGATION. CROSSING COULD ENDANGER THE EARTH." A cartoon of a terrified planet Earth holding out cloud hands in defense separated each iteration of the message. A few yards over, skis and snowboards jammed straight up in the snow marked the memorial for the ski/snowboard team that had died there in last year's avalanche. Someone must have returned early in the season to fix up the shrine, but the forlorn wind-damaged decorations indicated it had been months since anyone had come to pay their respects. Just as well.

The gray sky warned of the impending storm, but at least there wasn't any wind yet. The snow on the ground was pristine save for the occasional animal tracks. She resisted the temptation to throw herself flat and make a snow angel. Instead, she wandered closer to the pit, crossing the tape, to peer down at the man scraping the edge and pointing a scanner at the freshly exposed snow.

She waited while Mason finished taking measurements of the different layers of snow with a laser imager. Once he set the instrument aside, she cleared her throat. "Time to pack up. Weather Service says there's a storm coming."

Mason chuckled without humor. "This the same Weather Service that sent us here to see if last year's avalanche was caused by Global Fattening?"

Olivia crossed her arms and stepped back from the edge. She didn't trust the stability of the snow despite Mason's assurances. The rebar should have been installed further from the edge, but the Weather Service insisted they use only the roll of barrier tape it provided, and the congressionally mandated amount for this type of research wouldn't make a bigger circle.

She tried to explain about the possibility of the snow collapsing, but the Weather Service guy accused her of being "pro-plastics" and of wanting to waste taxpayer dollars. The thought still made her angry, especially since she couldn't tell which he thought was the worse insult.

She could have used some of the university's supply. They had some rolls bearing the message "LINE OF REASONING. DO NOT CROSS" that she found especially appropriate. But no; the Weather Service was adamant: only government-approved materials were to be used in the research. Otherwise, they'd invalidate the study—and the grant. Even more, the USWS representative was not going to approve more earth-endangering barrier tape.

She shrugged. "Hey, they're paying the university."

"Well, I hope they're okay paying for my answer. There's your avalanche." He pointed to a narrow horizontal band of roughly packed snow slicing through the smoother layers. "Weakened layer destabilized by last year's heavy snowfall. As for inciting factor, my money is on the Slay Bells."

"Sleigh bells?"

"Yeah, that ski/snowboarding team that disappeared last year? S-L-A-Y Bells. They came up here despite the warning markers; I'm betting they made too much ruckus at the wrong time and fwoom! No survivors."

Olivia shivered and scanned the barren mountainside again. It suddenly looked a lot less inviting. "They never did recover the bodies, did they?"

"Of course not. Why do you think I brought these with me?" He hefted out a Smith and Wesson "Unnatural Selection" Compensated Hunter pistol with laser scope from the blanket beside him. An equally impressive rifle lay waiting, along with some of the biggest bullets she'd ever seen.

She tsked and shook her head, but the weapons reassured her. "I should have known! You and your firepower. You read too many of those monster hunter books. Utah's clear—only a dozen sightings in what, the last decade?"

"I love those books. Besides, this is just a precaution. Trust me, I'd rather leave zombie hunting to the professionals, like my cousin Brook."

"I think they call it 'extermination.' Anyway, let's get out of here. Zombies or not, there's still a storm on the way. You can't shoot that."

Mason scanned gray sky on the horizon with the laser scope. "So much for the warm winter. Good conditions for the ski and snowboard contest, anyway."

He handed up his rifles, then the equipment. Olivia carefully gave him a hand as he pulled himself out of the pit. She thought she felt the snow give and stepped back fast.

Mason did, too, then paused. "What was that?"

Olivia listened, but all she heard was a distant shuffling. "Probably some animal preparing a shelter. Let's just get out of here." She slung one rifle over her shoulder, grabbed up the blanket, and started off to the snowmobile before he could protest. After a moment, she heard the snow crunch under his boots as he followed.

As their snowmobiles roared down the mountain, the snow on the uphill side of Mason's pit began to darken, and then crumble. Just below the avalanche strata, a gloved hand clawed out of the snow.

There were many times when Neeta felt snarky about Ted driving her van. Even though he'd been a stunt driver, she felt she was the better driver navigating the traffic of L.A. Out here, in the snowy, winding mountain roads of Northern Utah, however, she was glad to let him take the wheel.

"Are you sure we don't need chains?" Despite its width, the snow-covered two-lane highway twisted and curved as it rose. Steep mountains loomed to the left and sharp drops plummeted on the right. The clouds threatened snow, cut visibility, and made the evergreens look dark and bleak. She shivered despite the efficiency of her car's heater.

Ted reached over to squeeze her knee. "Take it easy, babe. We've got plenty of traction. Chains are for ice. This is nothing. I can't believe you haven't seen snow before, with all the traveling you did with your mom."

She resisted the urge to lean forward to see the road over the hood of her HumVan. He was right. She could hear the slush being kicked up by the tires.

She was doubly glad they were new. They'd just replaced them a couple of months ago. Running over zombies and the subsequent decontamination played merry havoc with the rubber. The bumper, too—she'd only had the car two years and was on her third front bumper. Spud had suggested she succumb to the inevitable and attach a cowcatcher. The idea tempted her.

Mind off work, Neeta, and relax. We're on vacation. She turned her attention back to the conversation. "We did, but Mom was on business. We flew into the closest airport, got driven to whatever exterminator conference or zombie regulations rally she was speaking at, and then we went home. I stopped going when I got to high school, anyway. But no. No long mountain drives in the snow. Mom's presentations were in the cities."

He gave her knee one last squeeze before returning his hand to the steering wheel. "Your mom was all about work."

"Well, the zombie syndrome was just becoming known—and there was so much misinformation then. Someone had to spread the message that zombies are pests, not people, and that they needed to be exterminated."

Ted lifted his fingers off the wheel in a shrug without actually letting go. "Oh, I know it was important work, but she could have taken an extra day or two with you to see the sights. I mean, who goes to London without seeing Big Ben? Or to DC without spending a day at the Smithsonian?"

"Or Utah without skiing?"

"Don't forget the Great Salt Lake. I'm not into the Great Salt Lake, although when we have kids, we have to go. My cousin Jordan took us when I was a kid, and we stuck our T-shirts in the lake and then let them dry standing up. It was awesome. They crackled and everything. Oh! And the Sundance Film Festival. That's always big. I've been twice—once when I filmed for African Maple, and again when I did stunts with Searching Dragon, Hidden Butterfly.

"I broke three bones in that one. Do you know how hard it is to leap gracefully between animatronic flowers while wearing butterfly wings? Not to mention fake breasts. Threw my center of gravity off. I don't know why Pat didn't do xer own stunts. Xe used to insist on it, and the whole movie was about xis gender transformation. And ninjas."

"Ninjas, of course."

"In pastel colors to blend in with the flowers. I wanted to be a ninja, but instead I had to wear fake breasts and butterfly wings because Pat's hormone therapy made xer feel frail. Then I had hang around Pat all of Sundance. You should have heard xer going on about the painful artistic process. I still had my ribs bound, and Pat was griping that xe broke a nail. Not my favorite film fest experience.

"Anyway, Sundance is on our list, too. I need an affirming experience."

Neeta snorted. "Yes, I've always wondered what tragic incident wounded your self-confidence."

Ted tried to answer earnestly but could not suppress the chuckle in his voice. "Still, it's true. I can't look at pastel ninjas—or fake breasts. You know how hard it is to avoid fake breasts in Southern California? Yet another reason to love you."

"Babe!" She felt her face heat.

"You're all real. I love that. But still. Sundance—on our list, with the Great Salt Lake."

"When we have time, Babe."

"When we make time, Babe. You Lyffe women are too much about work. That's gonna change now that you're the future Mrs. Lyffe-Hacker."

"I love that thought." Warmed now by something better than the car heater, she inhaled deeply and stretched to release the tension in her shoulders.

"Me, too," Ted said. "This vacation is going to be great. Plus, it'll be nice to do something non-extermination related. Who'd have thought you'd get a public appearance in Utah?"

"HumVans of Ogden requested us—me—but for once, it's all about the car." Some days, she regretted the deal she'd made with HumVans to advertise its vehicles, trading her reputation for one van outfitted for her zombie extermination business. She felt like a sellout. Yet after her last van had been destroyed in the zombie invasion of Burbank, she'd been desperate. She did love her new van, which was the envy of her exterminator friends, and the perks of being the Warrior Queen of the HumVan Scene did have perks.

"I have to remember to mention how well the van's handling the mountain roads," she told Todd.

Ahead of them, an electric sports car strained to keep speed on the steep grade. The GovMo Poise's red paint job and white racing stripe boasted power it obviously did not have. There was a reason people called it the Poser.

Their van was gaining on it. "Uh, Ted?"

Ted had warmed to his topic. "Absolutely. How cool is it that they want you to talk about the van? When you're posing in front of the van at the HotDogger competition, you can talk about the drive instead of the you-know-what's."

Her business-partner-and-fiancé said the last in a hushed voice. They'd agreed before they left that mentioning zombies might curse the trip, and that they would avoid the topic at all costs.

He continued, "Plus, with HumVans footing the bill, we'll have plenty of time and money for snowboarding. I can't wait to get my gnarl on!"

As usual, when Ted got excited, his foot got heavy on the accelerator.

"Slow down, Ted."

He turned to grin at her. "Oh, come on, how hard can it be? Hey, maybe I'll enter the contest, show them what a California surfer can do on their snow."

"Poser," she warned.

"What? Don't you think I can?"

"No, Poser!" Neeta pointed at the car in front of them. The oversized back end, patterned after the muscle cars of the twenty-teens, grew bigger as they gained. The license plate proudly declared "PR0GRES."

"Whoops!" Ted swerved into the other lane, hit the gas and swung back as an oncoming car flashed its brights, earning him angry honks from both the other drivers.

"Poser!" Ted shouted at the car receding in the rear-view mirror, adding a few swear words for good measure. "Leave it to Government Motors to make a sports car with a wimpy engine. I don't care how green it is. It's just missing the point!"

Neeta rested her head in her hands.

Ted spoke softly. "Sorry, babe. I'll keep my eyes on the road and my head off the slopes until we get there."

She willed her heart to stop pounding. "I'd like us to live long enough to have children."

"Gotcha, Boss. We have to think about the children! Eyes on the road, no taking out Posers...no jumping bridges?" His voice took on a teasing tone.

"Definitely no bridges. Jumping this van over the San Francisco Bay was bad enough." If they hadn't been rushing to help against a major zombie infestation, she'd have killed Ted that day.

"We only jumped a hundred and two feet of it. Besides, traffic on the working bridge was backed up. I had to take the Broken Bay Bridge."

She glared at him from the corner of her eye. He didn't acknowledge her look but kept his eyes forward and his face composed in innocent concentration until she couldn't take it any longer and snickered. He did make the job fun, even if she did want to strangle him for his antics sometimes.

"No jumps. If you have to be reckless this week, just do it because we're going after undead, okay?"

"Sh!" he hissed. "Don't mention the you-know-whats. You'll jinx it. This is a vacation. You, me, a couple of boards…"

"We do that in L.A. Most of the time, without the you-know-whats."

"Snuggling with hot cocoa before a warm fire in the fireplace?"

He smiled at her, his brows raised, and she got the jelly-legs feeling only he ever gave her. She savored it for a moment before chiding with a smile, "Eyes on the road."

"You got it, Boss. Hey, look. It's starting to snow."

Neeta turned her attention to the window, where large, fluffy flakes drifted down, and the world suddenly seemed peaceful and lovely.

Meanwhile, miles away from the road, but not far from where Mason and Olivia had dug their pit in the name of research, a woman screamed.

Chapter 3

A scream echoed across the mountainside, tearing through the peaceful, winter air. The trees at the edge of the wood shook, dislodging their snowy burdens. Jessica Zwelleger burst through, screeching as she dashed from their grasp. She ran full out, her boots sinking into the inches of newly fallen snow, arms pumping. She headed roughly in the direction of the shrine made of old skis and snowboards and Christmas-decorated mini-trees that memorialized the death of the Team Slay Bells, but she zigged and zagged, her hair flying as she whipped her head about, causing the fur-lined hood of her jacket to drop.

A figure staggered after her, his breath coming in ragged gasps.

She chanced a longer glance behind her, lost her footing, and fell. By the time she'd rolled over, her pursuer was nearly upon her. Arms outstretched, he leaned toward her and moaned. She held up her hands.

"All right! All right! I give up. You win again." Her shrieks turned into laughter, and she rolled in the snow, clutching her stomach and making no effort to calm her hysterics.

Ethan Pike flopped on the ground beside her and panted. What a run! He probably had enough stored energy to keep him warm for days. That was the awesome thing about his ski suit. It absorbed the energy of his movements and used it to keep him warm when he stopped. It converted sunlight into heat, too. He was like a walking solar panel or something. Which was totally cool, except for being warm. Anyway, the way Jessica was sweating, she would get chilly on the way home, and he'd be able to unzip his suit so she could warm her hands under it.

Yeah. Good run.

Once he got his breath, he reached in his jacket pocket and pulled out a fat twist of leaves and a lighter. He inhaled deeply and spoke with a hoarse voice. "See? Told you."

"Yep—a good run and a good toke. Better than Canablis." She sat up and pulled off her jacket, rubbing the fur over her sweaty neck before tossing it aside. Ethan watched in hormone-filled fascination.

He passed her the joint. She took a long drag, swaying slightly with pleasure. He tried not to drool.

She sighed. "I'm gonna pay for this when I get home. I'm supposed to be grounded for yelling at Mom. I wish she'd just let me buy this stuff instead of that over-the-counter shit."

"Anything's better than that over-the-counter shit. This shit is, like, pure, and you should always strive for purity because it's, you know, pure. Plus it's sexier." He sat up and leaned toward her, eyes closed, lips puckered.

She gave a little gasp and spun away from him, and he toppled. "Did you hear that?"

He pushed himself up, spitting out pure snow, and saw her hands were empty. "Hey! Where's that joint?"

She made vague waving motions in his direction as she headed toward an area blocked off with re-bar and neon ribbon with little cartoon earths on it.

He, too, could hear the moans, but dismissed them as he crawled around, swiping his gloved hands in a messy search pattern. "You lost it in the snow? Jeez, do you know how expensive those have gotten since the government started taxing them? My mom won't file an insurance claim for them for me, either. Stupid government with their stupid regulations and their stupid taxes... Wish it was illegal like in my dad's day..."

"Ethan, come here!" Jessica waved him toward the barrier. He grumbled as he rose, slipped, and finally got his footing. She laughed, but not at him. "Come on! You gotta see! This guy's like the abdominal snowman or something. Abombinable? Obamanble..?"

While she muttered through her search for the right word, he trudged to where she stood leaning against the barrier tape and looking into a ditch, his mind still on his joint. "You know, a good blunt is like a good man. You shouldn't… Hey, what's that guy doing?"

A lean, snow-covered man in a torn ski suit stumbled around the small, deep hole, bumping into the sides. He'd clawed at the frozen walls, but only succeeded at fraying his gloves…and the skin beneath. The walls bore bloody streaks.

Ethan couldn't take his eyes off the bloody walls. "Whoa, look at the lines. They're all, like pink. And awesome. Makes me want to paint. Do you want to paint the snow—you know, like Moab, but snow, not rocks? Still, like Moab. The colors, all streaky and pink… Moab in snow, you know?"

Jessica giggled. "Later, maybe. What's he doing, anyway? Hey, you! Stupid! What are you doing, anyway?"

The man stopped bumping himself against the wall and looked up and moaned, "Braaaiiins!"

"Yeah, you do need brains. How'd you get in there?"

Instead of answering, he began to claw at the snow under Jessica's feet. Distracted from his visions of Moab in Snow, Ethan laughed. He couldn't help it; the guy moved so slowly. What a moron!

"How'd you get in the hole?" Jessica kept asking. She stepped closer. The government ribbon strained as it tried to hold her back. She accepted its authority and bent over it instead. "Did you fall? Did you ski?"

"Skiiiiii!"

"Oh, hey, that's a good idea! Ethan, be a good blunt and get a ski from the shrine. We can pull him up."

"Why should I?"

"Please?" She turned to him with big eyes and pouty lips, and for a moment he was mesmerized by how beautiful the red lines in the whites of her eyes were, like the pink lines in the snow. He should paint her, all pink in the snow...

"Pretty please?"

"Yeah, yeah."

He spun on his heel and almost lost his balance at the edge of the hole. He clutched at the nearest rebar. While it kept him from falling into the pit, he still hit the ground, pulling the rebar down with him. It pushed out of the snow, causing part of the hole's wall to collapse.

Jessica shrieked. "You idiot! You're endangering the earth! Can't you read? Something horrible is going to happen now, I just know it. Stupid!"

Ethan felt a jolt of fear. Didn't his mother always tell him the government was never wrong, and he needed to listen to it? Then he remembered he never listened to his mother. "Yeah, whatever. It's not like I crossed the line, anyway. I just moved it. I'm going to find my joint. Dig him out yourself."

He tossed the rebar aside, or tried to; the safety tape caught and it flopped to the ground beside him. Jessica grabbed it. "Hey, yeah, we can use that! And then I can stay on this side of the tape. That's so genius. Ethan, you're a genius!"

"Whatever." Ethan sat up, dusting snow off his jacket, and caught a glimpse of ash downslope. He cheered. "My joint!"

While Jessica giggled and called encouragement to the trapped dude, Ethan crawled to his lost treasure. He brushed it off, relit it, and put it to his lips. Then, remembering how Jessica had lost it once already, he turned his back to her to finish his smoke in privacy. "Yeah, that's good stuff. Hey, that guy out yet?"

Jessica squealed, then screamed, "Help me, Ethan!"

There was a thump.

"You fall in? Klutz. Means you crossed the line! Give me a minute. Almost done." He took another drag while she screamed and gibbered. The other guy moaned.

"Hey, don't mess with my Jess!" he hollered without turning around. Yeah, better not to turn around. He could sound heroic and protective, but he didn't want to fight the guy or anything. He was a lover, not a fighter. Besides, what'd they teach them in school? If someone is being harassed, take decisive action by finding someone in authority. There wasn't anyone in authority for miles around, so what could he do? Not his fault.

Anyway, they'd moved on to slurpy noises. Guess she'd decided she liked it after all. Figures. Women were like joints. Fun for a while, then you had to get a new one. Didn't his grandma say that? And she'd had her hips replaced and everything…

He heard a rasping hiss and a moan, "Ethaaaan…"

Wait! Was that an…invitation? He nearly choked on his joint. He paused, took another toke and forced his voice into casual agreement.

"Fine. I've got an open mind, but save it for a hotel, all right? Come on. I got munchies. Nachos! Don't nachos sound awesome? Let's, like, get a room, order some nachos. You guys hungry?"

The Ute2 lodge was a huge, log-cabin style hotel and ski resort that nestled against the slope of the mountain, its A-frame portico opening to a ski lift mere yards away. With the room balconies draped in evergreens and lights, and the feathery snow falling, it looked to Neeta like a scene in a snow globe.

"Oh, Ted, it's delightful," she whispered with a breathy laugh. She could not bear to break the magic of the scene with the garishness of normal chatter.

Ted understood and replied only by squeezing her knee.

The moment was broken as they came across a life-sized doll of a skier smashed face first into a pole, its arms and legs sticking straight out on either side. The sign above it said, "Ski Aware!"

They burst into loud laughs.

Ted said, "So, want me to drop you off at the entrance with our stuff?"

She pointed to a spot not far from the doors. "There's the VIP parking. It's not far. Besides, I want to walk in the snow."

The chill air stung her cheeks, but it wasn't nearly as bad as she expected—less, in fact, than air conditioned restaurants before the California Carbon Footprint Reduction Act. She said as much to Ted as he pulled out their luggage.

He laughed. "The air's drier, so the cold doesn't stick. It'll bite when the wind picks up or when we're 'boarding down the slopes. We should buy ski masks, first thing."

The desk clerk gave them their keys and a note from the event coordinator to meet him at breakfast. The evening was theirs.

They had adjoining rooms with a door between them. Ted's opened to the slope, but Neeta's had the fireplace—and a Jacuzzi tub. She would definitely enjoy her vacation now! She opened her suitcase and started placing her clothes on hangers and in drawers.

Ted, naturally, tossed his bags in his room, then plopped down on her bed to watch her nest. "Wanna do mine next?"

"Maybe when we're married."

"Sounds good to me." He hopped off the bed and put his arms around her. "This is going to be an awesome vacation."

She leaned against him, eyes shut with contentment. "Mmm-hmm. A couple of hours showing off the van while we watch the ski contest."

He kissed her hair. "Otherwise, it's you me, some snowboards…"

"The fireplace…"

"And no—"

"Stop!" Neeta spun in his arms and pressed her fingers against his mouth. "Don't jinx it. We're here to advertise the van, not exterminate."

He chuckled. "Yet the van is fully loaded. You checked. Twice."

"After San Francisco, I will not be caught unprepared again. But we don't look for trouble, either."

"Trouble finds us no matter what, but I'm glad you're getting the idea." He gave her a long kiss.

"So, future Mrs. Lyffe-Hacker," he said when they'd pulled away. "There's still some daylight left. What say we get our jackets on and go strolling in a winter wonderland before dinner?"

"I think that sounds wonderful, future Mr. Lyffe-Hacker."

Ethan ran out of the meadow and into the woods, dashing around trees that, to his panicked and drug-addled mind, leaned toward him, branches reaching out to snatch him. His eyes widened, but he couldn't make sense of the twisting shadows. When he saw a clearing, he dashed toward it. An upraised root caught his foot. He tumbled down the rocky hill until he landed in a ditch and lay on his back, panting.

What had happened? Memories made a confused blur. Everything had been fine: He'd been toking, Jessica was getting it on with that guy. He'd suggested a hotel and nachos. Then someone put arms around him and he'd thought it was Jessica, kind of warmed up or something, but it was the guy and he couldn't pull away and then he...

Ethan put his hand to his neck. His glove came away bloody. What kind of perv..?

No matter. He'd gotten away. He had to be safe by now; the trees would have gotten the guy, right? Trees hate pervs. He'd heard that somewhere, hadn't he?

"Trees hate pervs." Yeah, sounded right.

Or maybe this was all a dream. Maybe he'd gotten some bad stuff, and this was just a dream. He lay against the bank, arms spread, and stared up at the falling snow. That was soothing. Yeah. He'd just wait 'till he was calm, then head down and get some help. Grandma wouldn't let him down.

"Ute2," he muttered so he'd remember. "Just get up, go to the Ute2, get some quality Ace. And nachos. Yeah."

He was still repeating it when his pulse at last stilled. The snow continued to fall, watched by dead eyes.

An Interview with Carol Lyffe, Zombie Exterminator

From the KSL archives

Saraeh Yeagi, KSL News 365: Carol, why don't Idaho and Utah see the same zombie problems other states do?

Carol Lyffe: There's no easy answer to that. Some of it is population demographics, some of it might be weather.

Still, if I had to narrow it down to the real differences, I'd say Geeks, Guns and Good Laws.

In the 20-teens Utah had a higher percentage of geeks than any other state in the nation, and a many of them were Walking Dead fans. I was a big fan myself. The series had its flaws, but one thing it did do well was show people that zombies were a threat and not misunderstood humans come back from the dead. Plus, Larry Correia, bestselling author of the Monster Hunter books, is a Utahan and had a big following in the state. So when the real zombie Not-pocalypse broke out, people there were primed to react in a way that protected the living. In other words, they kicked zombie butt.

Since Utah never banned guns in the state, they had the tools and training to take them out from a distance. The zombie contagion never had a chance to spread like it did on the coasts where gun control was more strict and there was—is—a concerted effort to try to integrate the rotters into society in hopes of rehabilitating them. That's why I am touring the nation this summer, to get across the message that you can't reform the undead.

Yeagi: The Not-pocalypse?

Lyffe: That's where Good Laws come in. Utah was one of the first states to institute spine severing as standard procedure after declaration of death. It's not really the spine, per se, of course, but all the nerves connecting the brain to the rest of the body. If a zombie can't move, it's not a real danger, unless someone's dumb enough to put his hand near its mouth or gets careless with decontamination or safe handling procedures. There have been accidents, or course, but the nearly worldwide implementation of this simple procedure has stopped what could have quickly become a runaway contagion.

You know, people talk a lot about finding a cure, but prevention is even more important. It's what kept the zombie contagion from sparking an apocalypse and instead created a problem trained professionals like myself can handle.

Yeagi: You just happened into this profession by circumstance, right?

Lyffe: I was already an exterminator, but the zombie part, yes. It was the 2020s; we still didn't know a lot about zombies. My partner, Jerry, and I thought we were seeing an unusual infestation of rats at a cemetery. We did not expect to come across a zombie hoard. We had to take them out with garden tools and extermination supplies.

Yeagi: How terrifying! What was going through your mind?

Lyffe: (Laughs) You mean other than the sheer disbelief and terror? I wasn't going to die there and leave my little girl all alone. It was me or the zombies, and I chose me. Fortunately, Jerry and I both saw combat in the Middle East, and we're damn good improvisers.

Yeagi: Thank you for your service. I understand that you were injured in battle?

Lyffe: (holds out her left arm) From the elbow down, this is fake, which saved my life when a biter almost got me. In fact, my daughter took that zombie out and saved my life in the process. That was her first rekill. She'll be a hell of an   exterminator   someday.

Chapter 4

Hambone bounded through the snow, the wide pads of his stubby legs leaving heavy footprints. He ignored the cold seeping into his belly. Girl was missing, and Master had tasked him to find her! He raised his head, seeking Girl's scent. The air stung his nose. Cold air brought the best smells.

He struggled up the snowdrift and paused, mouth open and panting, his breath making tiny clouds. His ears dragged in the snow, and he shook them, annoyed at the cold tips. He could hear his owner calling Girl, but he ignored it. He'd heard something else in a pit just ahead. A moaning, kind of like Girl's when she smelled so interesting and spent a lot of time in bed, eating chocolate and crying or yelling at Mistress.

Speaking of smells...

He galumphed to the open hole, thinking about the last time Girl pulled him into her lap and wrapped him in blankets while crying about how everyone smothered her.

Wowooo. He wished he could dig such a magnificent pit. Someone dug inside it, making it bigger. Maybe if he tilted his head and whined beseechingly, they'd let him help. Very few could resist his basset powers of persuasion. He crept forward.

Look! Girl!

He tilted his head to howl his discovery, then caught a new smell and stopped. It was Girl. It looked like Girl. It moaned like Girl. It smelled like Girl. Yet, it didn't. Girl didn't have pieces missing, or gurgle. Interesting, but not Girl.

The scent was of dead meat.

He tilted his head, whining in confusion. Girl/Not Girl stopped clawing at the side of the pit and twisted slowly. "Haaaam!" She/Not She held out her arms.

Hambone skittered back, a snarl rising to his lips before his doggie brain registered. Definitely Not Girl! Not alive!

Master should not see this. Master wouldn't like it. No, no. And Master was not fun when he was mad. If Hambone couldn't find Girl, he needed to find something else for Master. He left the moaning Not Girl and headed up the hill.

Find a something, find a something....

There was a new smell! What could it be? It was kind of people and kind of rotten hamburger... Definitely not of Girl. Oh, he had to find it! It would be good, he just knew it.

He stretched out his nose. It was close, maybe even under the snow, close. Find the smell. Find the smell. He moved further up the hill, sniffing, ignoring the exasperated cries of his master. Hambone always came back, and when he brought something new and interesting to present, the Master was happy. The Master would put it on the Mistress' sewing table and laugh while she shrieked. The more she shrieked, the better Hambone's reward. He'd get something grand this time, for sure! Then Master wouldn't get mad about Girl/Not Girl.

He heard another sound, a muffled moan from under the snow. Wowoo! Found it! He tilted his head back, baying, and was rewarded by a sharp, commanding call of his name. Now the Master knew! He ignored the call but galumphed toward the other sound. The smell came from that direction. The snow moved. He paused, head tilted, then perked. Something blue was under it. Blue and moving.

Hooray—toy!

With scurrying legs, he dug up the prize and grasped it with his teeth. It resisted at first. Tug-of-war! Hambone loved tug-of-war. He braced his legs and pulled. The toy's groaning turned to growls, and he growled back. Mine, mine!

A rip and a wafting of rotten hamburger smell, and it was his. Just in time, too—the gentle snowfall had started to get icy. Now that he had discovered the Not Girl and won a prize for the Master, he wanted to curl up in front of the warm fire and get belly rubs. He turned his back on the groaning creature, spread his legs, and piddled so all the world would know of his victorious presence.

He trotted back toward his master, his mouth full of his prize—a partly rotted arm in a blue jacket sleeve, its blue-gloved fingers curled with the middle one extended in a universal symbol of anger and defiance.

He didn't find Girl, but he had something to present the Master. Wouldn't his master be proud?

Neeta bolted upright in bed, a scream choking her throat, her heart pounding. She blinked her eyes furiously to remove the vision of Donald Eidelberg's severed head popping out of the trophy she was presenting the winning skier. When she could see the shadows of the hotel room around her, she released the breath she held. Bringing her legs up to her chest, she leaned her head against her knees.

It was ridiculous! He's not the first person she'd seen die on the job. He wasn't even the first contaminated person she'd beheaded. Why did he have to keep haunting her dreams, and why now? She hadn't dreamed about him in months, not since she and Ted got engaged.

I have got to get past this before I get married. I am not having a screaming nightmare on my honeymoon!

In the meantime, it was 4:30, and she knew from experience she wouldn't get back to sleep. In the next room, Ted snored. Something else she'd have to get used to, although her mom had snored loud enough to be heard throughout the house. In fact, it had taken Neeta a couple of months to get used to the quiet after she died.

"Oh, Mom, I wish you could have met Ted. You'd have loved him."

She hugged her knees, feeling just a little alone. She was the only child of a single mom who herself had grown up in foster care. She had no idea who her birth father was. With Mom gone, she didn't have any family…

Where'd that thought come from? She shook herself. She had the Lees; they'd treated her like a daughter since she and Min had shared a playpen. The Hollermans. Jason always called her his "Little Girl." Ted's family was…odd…but it was huge.

"It's Bergie," she said aloud. "All that family at his funeral. And now the wedding. Still, this is stupid. What did you always say, Mom? You can sit around feeling sorry for yourself, or you can look around and see all the good things, and then get up and do something about what's bothering you."

She wiped her damp cheeks and let out a cleansing breath. She'd had the best mom in the world, and she was marrying the best guy ever. She loved her job, and—she laughed—she got a free ski vacation to Utah because of it.

Yeah, Bergie had become zombie food, but the other Zombie Death Extreme plebes survived, and even thrived. LaCenta had just scored her sixth re-kill, and Lacey and Spud's twins were already crawling.

"They're never still. They take after their mom that way," Pippin (a.k.a. Spud) had told her, and he hadn't stuttered once their whole conversation.

Gordon and Nasir received medals from the Afghan government for their work against the undead there, and Ted—well, she had a partner in more ways than one with Ted.

Feeling better, she took a hot shower and sat in front of the fireplace in her favorite white bathrobe while she read up on the charity she was helping promote with the event, Operation Homefront.

Mom loved this charity. She'd been injured when a mine blew off half her arm. She never told Neeta the details, even when she was dying of cancer. All she'd say was, "I didn't even know I was pregnant. Thank God, you were all right." Nonetheless, she'd needed extensive surgeries, complicated by the fact that she refused to abort Neeta. Even with the military paying for the new arm, it added up. It was Operation Homefront's help, combined with an anonymous donation, that let her manage her bills and purchase the cottage in Inglewood where Neeta still lived and ran the family extermination business.

Neeta felt a little closer to her mom for being able to talk up the charity.

A knock interrupted her studies. "Babe, can I come in? You decent?"

Her mouth opened to automatically invite him in; then, she remembered she didn't have anything on under her bathrobe. "Give me a minute to get dressed."

"Okay, but dress warm. We need to go eat and talk to that event guy. Then, it's snowboarding lessons time!"

Sheriff Rourke halted his snowmobile at the edge of the avalanche area. The sun had crested the mountains, bathing the field in brilliant light, but he couldn't stop a feeling of foreboding. Last year, an avalanche had killed seven people here. This year, it looked like some of those seven were returning as undead…unless some sicko was digging them up and mutilating them. "Winter wonderland—right. Where'd you say Hambone found the arm?"

Gunther dismounted his own machine, but leaned against it, arms crossed, scowling. "I didn't. Hambone and I were looking for that no-good daughter of mine, and he ran off after a smell. But it was obviously Flip's arm, so it had to have come from here."

Rourke swore under his breath. "You didn't show it to Connie, did you?"

"Cut me some slack. Even I have my limits. I took it straight to you."

"Miracles never cease."

"Shut up. We were looking for Jessica. She still hasn't shown up at home."

Rourke paused in mid-dismount. "You think she might be around here?"

"Hell if I know. She and Connie got into it again over that doping boyfriend of hers. For all I know, they're heading to Vegas for a quickie wedding." Gunther's gloved hands clenched and unclenched against the desire to strangle someone.

Rourke hoped he was right. He'd rather deal with a domestic problem than a zombie any day. Angry dads could be reasoned with. "All right. We'll keep an eye out, and I'll call in an Amber Alert when we get back. At least it hasn't snowed heavy up here yet."

He saw some small indents and pointed. "Those look like dog tracks. Let's see where they head. We probably should walk from here on out. You go that way, and we'll cover more ground. Take this walkie-talkie; the last thing we want to do is yell. Still, keep in sight."

"Oh, no. We are not splitting up." Gunther ignored the walkie-talkie Rourke held out to him, heaved himself off the snowmobile he'd been leaning on, and pulled his shotgun from the case strapped to the side of the vehicle. "Ain't you seen that Marcel Chelemas video? 'If you ain't severed the head...'"

"'Don't assume it's dead.' Yeah, yeah. We have it at the office."

"We had a copy at home until Connie heard what Chelemas did to Neeta Lyffe. She threw the DVDs into the fireplace and deleted all our copies, even the one we stuck in the basement with the emergency food and water. Now, she wants to buy that zombie survival video from that Trelan Billiot guy. Probably be the same stuff, too. I told her there was nothing wrong with the Chelemas vids, but she said after hearing how he attacked Neeta, Cajun accents are a trigger. That woman's got more triggers than all my guns combined."

"It's a wonder you're still with her."

"Hey! I love that woman, flaws and all. But we were talking about you and me not splitting up, and you know what Chelemas says about that? He says, 'If you think there's a zombie around, stick togeth-er...'"

"'...unless the other guy is some coyoun who'll get you killed.' Right. Good point. You a coyoun?"

"I don't even know what that means, but I do know you won't get me killed. Don't worry about me. I did six months in the Spratly Islands. I know what a human looks like. I care."

Rourke gave the expected chuckle at the joke all Spratly Island War veterans shared. In 2037, America joined France and several Pacific nations to protect the various Spratly Islands against invasion—not by a single nation, but against an international environmental terrorist group, Sea Turtles and Friends. SeaTAF had been determined to drive all humans off the islands and kill those who refused to leave, all in the name of protecting the endangered species in the area. In the world's first war against an environmental group, the allied nations were as concerned about protecting the at-risk animals as they were about securing the islands. Hence, the joke: Show you care! Shoot the humans, not the turtles.

"Fine, but just remember: zombies can look human until they bite you. Be careful."

Gunther loaded two shells and pumped the gun with a firm jerk. "I'll do a warning shot at the feet if I have any doubts."

They made their slow way up the slope, following the tracks, Rourke taking lead and Gunther following, mostly looking back and to the sides. The crunching of the snow under their feet sounded too loud in the still air, but at least that was the only unnatural sound. Still, how well did zombies hear? Would they be drawn to their footsteps?

Gunther had similar thoughts. "You know, I'm wondering if watching some zombie defense video is really the best training for this. Maybe we should call some exterminators?"

Rourke was tempted. However, that would take a lot of time, and even though he didn't want to say it to Gunther, he didn't think Jessica would run off to Vegas. He'd known her since she was in diapers, and she was more level-headed than her parents gave her credit for, despite her wild side and idiot boyfriend. A run in the woods was more her style. "Nearest one's Salt Lake. It's not like we ever had a problem 'round here."

"Great. You see anything? This place is creeping me out." Gunther scanned the horizon.

Me, too. Rourke didn't voice the thought, but his back itched with the surety that a one-armed, blue-suited corpse of a skier was heading their way, intent on a breakfast of brains. He was sure he heard some kind of thumping from somewhere, but sound carried a long way in the mountain air. He fought against the urge to shout Jessica's name.

If she was out here, he could only hope she'd found some hole to hide in.

He thought he saw a disturbance in the snow and headed toward it, gun out and ready. Nothing alive or otherwise leapt out at him, but there was a large messy hole, some ripped flesh, and a circle of yellow snow. Erratic, half-smeared tracks led downhill.

Rourke swore. He'd hoped he'd find a half-trapped corpse he could treat to a double-tap and be done with it. "Yeah, that's where Hambone got his prize. Careful where you step now; there's gore uphill and to the left. Looks like Flip dug himself out and headed that way. Come on, let's see if we can find him."

"He's moving downhill? Let's go back, get the snowmobiles."

"I dunno. What if the others are still below the surface? We might stir up the snow and unearth them. Besides, this is still a no-vehicle zone after the avalanche." He didn't comment on the wisdom of firing their guns. He'd risk being buried in snow to being bitten by a zombie any day.

Rourke chewed his mustache as he did a slow 360, surveying the surroundings and straining to hear anything out of the ordinary. Silence rewarded him.

Meanwhile, Gunther was focused on the edge of the woods. Rourke could guess what he was thinking. His house was always full of conflict, with a teenage daughter and that hormonal boyfriend of hers causing trouble, and his wife, Connie, going through The Change. Walks in the woods with Hambone were all the peace Gunther got. Now that had been taken from him, too.

More importantly, Jessica loved the woods.

Rourke wished he had some words of reassurance, but he never made promises he couldn't keep.

He pointed to the tracks leading away from the mess. At least Flip had not gone toward the woods…from here, anyway.

"I think he headed this way." Without waiting, he started forward. Downslope and to the right was a circle of rebar, half of which had toppled. Something to the left caught his eye. He picked up his pace, praying he was mistaken.

Behind him, Gunther said, "Know what? I take back what I said about reinforcements. We've got guns, and we're both good shots. You're the sheriff. Screw the No Vehicle zone. Let's get the snowmobiles, call in a potential zombie, and go hunting ourselves. It's a half-frozen zombie—it can't have gone far. Hey, wait up!"

Rourke spun fast and sprinted to his friend, stopping him before he took too many steps downhill. He grabbed Gunther's arm and propelled him back the way they came.

"Gunther," Rourke commanded, his voice low and hoarse, "I want you to take your snowmobile and head back down. As soon as you're in cell phone range, call the sheriff's office. Tell them to call Salt Lake for a Z-Mat team ASAP, then you send some deputies back here to the Slay Bells memorial."

"Who's the coyoun now? We're not splitting up."

"Gunther! Do what I say, and don't look back."

"Oh, hell! Why'd you have to say that? What do you see?" He broke away and was down the hill before Rourke could stop him. "No. No!"

A white jacket with a tan faux-fur trim lay on the ground. Uphill of that, blood darkened the snow in messy splotches. They could just make out two trails of blood leading toward the woods on the other side of the clearing. They didn't go very far before the snow had covered them too thickly to see.

"Jessica!" He lunged forward, but Rourke snagged him.

"Hush!" he hissed. "That might not be hers. Listen to me. I'll keep searching, but one of us has to get down the mountain and warn people. Look!" He pointed past the carnage.

At the shrine of skis and snowboards, only a single ski remained.

Chapter 5

Ted planted the back of his snowboard into the snow and regarded the bunny slope with a sour face.

"I am so done with shredding with toddlers."

Neeta smacked his arm with the back of her gloved hand. "Don't be like that. Look!" She placed a finger under his chin, directing his attention toward the horizon.

Last night's storm had coated the area in pristine white, unbroken save for the ski tracks. The evergreens drooped under their snowy burdens, the green of the boughs rich in contrast with the white. Even the bare brown branches of scrubby bushes had a certain charm under the pillows of snow. Farther into the distance, the greens transformed to a blue-gray, and the mountains cut a stark outline against the clear blue of the sky.

"I didn't think anything could be as beautiful as the ocean," Neeta said.

"Oh, I can think of something."

Neeta met Ted's blue eyes, blushed, and leaned into him. He put his arm around her. She loved that he said that kind of stuff now, loved hearing it more than she had any other time in her life. Funny how much getting engaged had changed them.

"Bet I know where the view's even better…" he sing-songed.

He twisted so that they both looked up the hill. The very steep hill. Neeta's heart jumped just thinking about it.

Some things about her man would never change.

"I'm not ready for that. We've only had the one beginner lesson."

"Right—so you know the basics. The rest is just practice, and we should do it on a more challenging slope. The sun's almost overhead; the lighting will change if we wait. Come on, look at that kid—he's what, six, maybe eight, and he's doing fine."

The boy in a red-and-green snowsuit and helmet headed toward them, tracing a gentle serpentine trail in the snow. Arms at his side and relaxed, he did make it look easy—and fun.

"All right!" Neeta laughed. "Let's go before I change my mind."

They snatched up their boards and headed to the lift. Ted paused at the glass-encased map attached to a pole. He traced a green line.

"See? If we keep to our left, we can take 'Cupcake.' How hard can Cupcake be?"

"I guess I can handle Cupcake."

On the lift, however, Neeta felt her doubts resurface.

"Future Mrs. Lyffe-Hacker, you're not afraid of heights, are you?" Ted asked after she'd puffed out a huge breath for the second time, hoping he wouldn't notice. He draped his arm across the back of the seat and caressed her shoulder.

"No. Maybe, a little. Hope my knee is up to all this." It twinged, bringing the memory of hanging off a catwalk, her ligaments torn, contemplating a ten-foot drop onto hard cement and a horde of radical environmentalist zombies. She scooted a little deeper into the seat.

Ted hugged her closer. "Doc said your knee is good as new. Is that really it? You had another nightmare last night, didn't you?"

She looked toward a hotdogger taking a mogul-riddled slope in tight, energetic turns, but her mind had returned to the nightmare: bleachers full of avid skiing fans who were all shouting, "Murderer!" Bergie's severed head inside that trophy, asking her "Why'd you do it, baby?" She'd rather fall fifteen feet into zombies than face that.

"You know, I talk about it enough to Dr. Rose," she snapped at Ted.

Ted took his arm from around her. "Okay, Boss. But I'm here if you want a different perspective. For now, maybe we should put our minds to getting off the lift?"

They winced as the seat ahead of them booted a skier dismounting too slowly, sending him tumbling.

With one foot strapped to their snowboards and one free, they managed to exit the lift and get to the staging area without incident. Neeta made sure her board was perpendicular to the slope, then set her foot in the other straps.

"Hey, babe. Think we should apply a little surfer tradition and bow to the mountain?"

"I'm not sure that's a good idea." Neeta straightened from fixing her strap just as Ted yelped in surprise, and she saw him speeding backward, to the right, on a blue marked slope called "Slippery Lip."

"Ted!" Without thinking, she twisted to see him better, and then she was sliding down Slippery Lip herself.

The cold wind bit at her face, making her regret pulling off the ski mask. Her feet, still used to working a surfboard, twitched inside the boots. She shifted her weight and teetered. With a jerk, she caught her balance, overcompensated, and caught it again.

Ted meanwhile, whooped and hollered as he sped down the mountain, bouncing over moguls, barely missing other skiers, and managing to conquer the slope without knowing what he was doing.

Some days, she hated the charmed life he led.

She blew air out of puffed cheeks and forced her mind to the lesson: neutral stance, feet under body, small movements. She resisted the urge to press the edge of her board against the snow, despite the fact that trees, bumps, and other skiers flashed past her. She would catch up with Ted. Still, she kept her center of mass on the board as she turned; no way would she match Ted's dynamic and showy turns. If she didn't know he hardly had any idea what he was doing, she'd have accused him of showing off.

Actually, no—he was showing off. She just hoped he didn't kill himself in the process.

"Ted! Ramp!" She pointed toward the snowy incline on his path. In her inattention, she hit a mogul that bumped her into the air. She squealed as the board landed, jarring her knees.

He gave her a thumbs up.

"No! Ted!"

Too late. With a skid that sent snow spraying, he angled himself up the ramp. He hit it fast, soared...

He grabbed his board...spun...

...lost his center of gravity...

...and landed on his back with a thud she could hear.

"Ted!"

Neeta dug the edge of her board into the snow as she got to him, causing her to topple over beside him. Snow got under her collar and sent cold spikes down her back, but that was nothing compared to chill of seeing her fiancé groaning on the ground, arms splayed, the edge of the board partly dug into the snow. She sat up and tried to scoot herself closer. "Ted, babe, are you okay?"

He twisted his head toward her, grinning. "Okay, so no bowing to the mountain—but you have got to try that ramp! I felt like a snowbird." He waved his arms and made cooing sounds.

"You!" She grabbed a handful of snow and hurled it at him. "Seriously, are you all right?"

"Sure." He grunted as he lifted his legs, freeing the board, and sat up. "A little winded, but I know how to take a fall. I was a stuntman, you know. Besides, it's not like I was leaping off a toadstool to get smacked by an animatronic petunia."

"You broke bones. I thought your specialty was cars."

"Hello? Animatronic petunias! It was just the one time. I'm awesome with stunts. Cars… that's another story. I wasn't that good with cars."

"What? But my van! The Broken Bay Bridge!"

He kept talking as if putting their lives in danger in a stunt jump last summer had been an audition. "I know, right? I usually don't do that well with cars but falls! Love a good tumble." He set his gloved hand on hers. "As for you, future Mrs. Lyffe-Hacker, not bad for your first day on the slopes."

He jerked his head up the mountain. She gasped as she looked up the slope that seemed more a steep bumpy incline with no discernible easy path. She gulped. "I'm so glad I was not thinking about that on the way down."

Ted worked at his strap to free one foot and stood. "Yeah, well, don't think too hard the rest of the way down, then, and you'll be awesome."

Neeta glanced down a hill just as a snowboarder collided with a skier, sending poles flying. "Great." She plastered a smile on her face and held out her hand for Ted to pull her up.

He accepted her hand, but not her façade. "You know, for someone who owns her own chainsaw workout course and is so awesome on the waves, you're awfully shy about trying a new sport."

"I grew up exterminating. Mom taught me to defend myself against you-know-whats when I was seven. I took surfing lessons because Min was doing it, too."

"Well, our kids will be different. Hackers have adventurous genes. I'm all about new things. You going to be okay with that?"

She suddenly had a vision of him taking their 16-year-old son to some test track for a driving lesson. It's just a little ramp, babe... The mad glee on their boy's face would match his father's. "Actually, that's one of the things I love about you, future Mr. Lyffe-Hacker. Besides, we have to think of the children."

He grinned. "So, down to the lift and try Cupcake this time?"

He was so cute, with mischief sparking in his eyes and his snow-damp hair sticking out at all angles from his helmet—and her back was freezing from the snow that had gotten under her coat. "How about back to my room for hot cocoa and a fire, then later, we take an advanced lesson?"

His grin widened, making her heart skip. Just then, a skier in the red parka of the ski patrol stopped beside them. "You guys really shouldn't stop below the ramp," he chided. "Hey, wait a minute—are you Neeta Lyffe and Ted Hacker, the zombie exterminators?"

"Does that get us out of trouble or into it?" Ted quipped, but the man had pulled out his walkie-talkie.

"This is Mark on Slippery Lip. I found them. We'll be there in ten." He stuck the walkie-talkie back into his fanny pack, waved someone to go around the jump, and grasped his pole. He dug the tips into the ground a couple of times, twisting the baskets into the snow, a nervous gesture to Neeta's eyes.

"We've been looking for you for an hour. Would you follow me, please? There are some folks in the lodge that need to see you."

She couldn't fake the same confidence for Mark as she had for Ted. "I'd like to follow, but I'm not sure how well I'll follow. This is our first day. We hit this slope by accident."

"You've done the worst of it. Just take it easy and slow and you'll do fine. If we get separated, we'll meet at the green doors." He pushed off then, but skied in slow, easy curves.

"Come on! Bet there's a camera crew wanting to interview you!" With a whoop, Ted leaned in and sped down the hill.

From the worried look on the ski patrolman's face, however, Neeta had her doubts that anything good waited inside the green doors.

Mark led Neeta and Ted in silence to the manager's office on the third floor of the lodge. The small, paneled room had just enough space for some shelves, a desk, a couple of file cabinets, and two chairs. With the manager, the sheriff, and a large, unkempt man who could not hold still, there was hardly enough room for Neeta and Ted to squeeze in. Mark accepted the manager's thanks and left, closing the door behind him.

The manager reached across the table to shake their hands. "Burton Witherspoon. This is Sheriff Rourke Buttuns and Gunther Zwelleger. A pleasure to meet you—or it would be, under different circumstances." He offered her a chair, causing the large man to huff impatiently. That was enough to tell Neeta what the manager hadn't gotten the nerve to say. She bit back a sigh and waved off the chair. So much for vacation.

"Where did you see them—and how many zombies are we dealing with?"

The sheriff set his LawDroid on the desk and pulled up a map of the area. "At least two, maybe as many as nine. We're not sure. We have positive identification on a severed arm, and some fresh blood and flesh—sorry, Gunther—here." He circled an area a couple of miles uphill from the ski resort. "We're still running DNA tests, but the arm most likely belonged to a Flip Johnson, a snowboarder who died in an avalanche last year. The blood…well, we're not sure…"

The large man pushed between them. "Look, my daughter is out there. You guys are the experts at this! We need to get you out there, chopping these things down and finding her! Now let's go!"

"Gunther, calm down," the sheriff said, but Gunther didn't listen. Neeta got the feeling the sheriff had said those words more than once to the distraught father.

Gunther ignored him. "What do you need? Just tell me what you need and let's get out there!"

"Easy!" Neeta set her hand on his bicep. "Easy. First, we need some information—that way we don't just charge around blindly, okay? Zombies are essentially mindless, but they always have some residual thought processes that can help us predict what they might do. Anything you can tell us about their personalities or habits in life will help us predict their possible actions in death."

"We have all our equipment in the van," Ted added as he studied the map, "but I don't see any roads."

"Nah, it'll be snowmobiles," the sheriff replied.

"Okay, so we need backpacks and some way to carry our boards. Neeta, you get the intel while Gunther and I prep?"

She nodded, schooling her face into professional neutrality. She loved how Ted jumped in to give Gunther something constructive to focus on other than his daughter. Ted could be so good with people!

"Grab me a dry shirt." The snow had melted under her jacket, and she was damp and distinctly uncomfortable. When the door closed, she turned back to the map. "What are the chances his daughter's been bitten?"

"We found her coat near the scene, but it was clean. She went missing last night. I was going to stay and look for her, but Gunther wouldn't leave to get help, so we came together. We were just here to commandeer some gas for the snowmobiles and ask around on the off-chance she might have come here last night, when Burt told us you about you. I've got a couple of deputies en route, and SLC Z-Mat is on their way."

"There's hope then, but if she's bit, she's dead by now. She'll have to be rekilled. Gunther cannot be part of the search." She hated saying it, but she hated the thought of a father confronting his zombiefied daughter even worse. She knew the horror of killing someone she cared about. "You said nine possible?"

Sheriff Buttuns eyed the door, chewing on his mustache as if thinking about how he was going to keep the determined father from the search.

Burton answered. "Flip was part of a group of seven competitors, the Slay Bells. They were here for last year's Ute2/Operation Homefront HotDogger competition and decided to do some extreme night skiing in a restricted area. There was an avalanche. We never found the bodies—until Gunter's dog came home with Flip's arm, anyway. Oh, man! Should we put Hambone to sleep?"

Neeta shook her head. "The pathogen doesn't spread to animals—only humans. So possible seven skiers, the girl and...a boyfriend?" It followed cliché.

The sheriff nodded. "Ethan Pike, 17. Busted a few times for petty theft, driving under the influence. My guess is that the blood is his. If he saw a zombie, he'd be too high to notice."

"The girl, too?" Neeta asked. The sheriff shrugged. "Okay, we might be able to draw them out with some smoke, loud music, and a hibachi. In the meantime, send Gunther home to get his wife and any other family members out of the house. Have someone guard the place, just in case—someone armed for zombies. Most teen zombies head home—after that, boyfriend's, best friend's, or places they frequent often. Schools, sometimes. Get a list and have Gunther warn folks if you think he's up to it. It'll give him something constructive to do. Tell me about the skiers— locals?"

The manager shook his head. "Flip's from Salt Lake; Tom and Muchelle Spars, Colorado; Morton Bellringer, Montreal somewhere; and Crown Spillanger, Montana. Pender Byways was from Vegas, but spent most of the winter here. Flannelette Sew-enge…no one really knows; she just rode the circuit, disappeared in summer, and marked her home as 'Boardertown,' B-O-A-R-D. They didn't have a particular hangout or anything, just came together for the contest," Burton said.

"That means they'll be heading for the slopes. How heavy is the snow up there? It might slow them down."

The sheriff sighed and crossed his arms. "They had skis."

"Zombies? On skis?" Ted's squeal came loud and clear over her helmet as they followed the sheriff on snowmobiles up to the accident scene. "If it weren't so dangerous, it'd be core awesome!"

"Apparently, there was some kind of shrine set up with skis and snowboards. This won't be easy. They were already fearless and skilled. Now they're mindless, fearless and skilled—and the only thing that connects them to the area is that ski contest." Neeta spoke through chattering teeth. Even with all the layers she could pile on under her HazMat suit and her ski mask making her helmet uncom-fortably tight, the cold air cut through her. The

January ocean seemed like a warm bath by comparison.

"And Ski Dummy," Ted said, referring to the large doll or a skier that had crashed into a pole. "Apparently, Pender hated that thing, and we know what a motivation that can be in death."

"True." Earlier this year, they'd taken on a hoarde of radical environmentalist zombies intent on destroying the Waysterman refinery as a protest against manure-based fuels. She'd never known anyone could be so against crap. "I can't believe the lodge owner – Brown was his name? – won't just take it down."

"It's historical."

"It's a dummy! He could put it up later, anyway."

"Ours is not to reason why," Ted said philosophically. "Ours is to behead stuff and get paid. We've marked the area and set traps. With any luck, we'll take Pender out before he goes after the dummy, anyway."

Luck? How could Ted talk about luck the way her life had been going lately? "Are you sure you want to marry me? I'm cursed."

Ahead, Sheriff Buttuns swerved to avoid a root that arched out of the snow, and she followed. She heard a thump and guessed that Ted chose to jump the branch instead.

"Nah. You're interesting. I love that. Besides, it's got to be easier than a surfing zombie. At least if we wipe out, we won't drown. Come on. If it weren't for your so-called curse, we wouldn't be snowmobiling in restricted territory right now. How fuze is that? And just a few days ago, we got to surf an off-limits beach. It's like getting to taste the forbidden fruits of life."

"Isn't eating forbidden fruit what got Adam and Eve kicked out of Eden?"

"Don't be a downer, babe. We get to break rules on official business. Just go with it. 'Embrace the suck,' as Gordon used to say."

Gordon had been a Marine who had been discharged for too much enthusiasm. "I'm not a Marine."

"Your mom was. Doesn't any of that rub off?"

"Shrapnel shredded her arm. She was medically discharged before I was born."

"You need to get into the spirit of this. Sing with me: Oh, the zombies outside are frightful/but the napalm's so delightful…"

"You're insane! I'm marrying a crazy man." Even so, she couldn't keep the smile out of her voice. He did make the job fun.

"As long as you love me so…"

Competitive Skier Arrested for Harassing a Static Display

Feb 18, 2043. Storm's Brunt, UT: Competitive skier Pender Byways has been arrested and charged with vandalism, resisting arrest and hate speech infractions after an altercation involving a static display at the Ute2 ski lodge.

Police were answering a call about someone shouting obscenities and discovered Byways dancing around the Ski Dummy, well-known Ute2 landmark, shaking a can of spray paint and shouting "Loser!" among other profane and emotionally hurtful phrases. Allegedly, Byways had also urinated on the display and was still pulling up his ski pants at the time of arrest. Byways had a blood alcohol level of .13.

Byways body slammed two officers while spraying a message on Ski Dummy and pulling up his pants, according to the police report.

"It was actually a pretty impressive feat of coordination," said one of the officers on the scene who asked not to be named. "You can see why he's such a force on the slopes."

Ski Dummy is a manikin of a skier crashing into a pole, reminiscent of those Halloween display witches that looked like they crashed into trees. The witch displays, of course, were banned after being declared hate speech against wiccans and Quiddich players. Above Ski Dummy's head is the sign saying, "Ski Aware."

Byways was in the process of painting "LoozR" on the sign.

"It's a humorous way to remind people to be careful on the slopes," said Altimeter "Tim" Brown, owner of the Ute2 ski resort. The resort is hosting the first annual Operation Homefront/Ute2 HotDoggers Ski and Snowboard Competition, in which Byways is competing as part of the Team Slay Bells. Brown said he'd consider dropping the charges once Byways sobered up.

"This contest is about raising money for charity," he said. "Though if it happens again, I will take legal action."

Byways is planning some legal action as well. In a statement released by his lawyer and agent, the competitive skier said he would sue Ute2 for having such a display. "It's totally insulting to us skiers. I mean, what kind of loser skis into a tree?"

Chapter 6

Neeta parked her snowmobile beside the sheriff's and spent a few moments studying the area. Not the bloody snow and ruined memorial, time for that later, but the dark blue-grey forests stark against the white ground, mountains rising to meet a blue sky where clouds had started to gather. This is what she wanted to remember, the rugged beauty of the place, not the mess she and Ted had been hired to clean up.

Without the breeze from the snowmobile, she felt so much warmer. What a relief. She inhaled deeply, letting the cool sharp air fill her lungs— then coughed when it stung. That was all right; it just added to the newness of the experience. She heard the sharp cry of a raptor and looked up to see several birds circling overhead in the direction of the memorial.

When Ted pulled up, giving his engine one extra roar before turning it off, she pointed to them. "Bet we find something that way." She dismounted and dug into the storage area under the saddle of the snowmobile to exchange her ski gloves for the knit ones she could wear under her work gloves. Her fingers might get cold, but she didn't want to risk taking time to change them when they actually saw a corpsicle. "Corpsicle" was a time-honored term for zombies, especially those encountered in the winter, but never had it seemed more appropriate than for one that dug itself out of the frozen ground.

While the Sheriff went to check on the deputy who waited by the desecrated memorial, Neeta and Ted loaded their belts with tools of the trade: napalm and antihistamine grenades to take any shamblers out at a distance, and cans of Red Bull and some recent ski magazines they'd gotten from the lodge gift shop to draw the zombies to them. Even though bleach water would not freeze in the squirt guns, they decided against bringing any. The snow would make it relatively ineffective on cold dead bodies. They both had small spray bottles of the stuff, however. In case of an approaching corpsicle, they could dowse themselves or the officers to repel the zombie. Finally, Neeta attached her monofilament sword to its hook on her belt.

Ted, however, stepped away from the snowmobiles and activated his. The monofilament unfolded at the press of the button, and the electric field around it charged, glowing and emitting a clean hum in the still air. He did a few swings, then pointed it to the ground, causing the snow to sizzle as he swiped it in a pattern.

"Ted, what are you doing?" Neeta walked around her snowmobile to see that he'd drawn a heart with TH + NL in a snowbank.

"Just wanted to be sure it works in the snow itself. You know, just in case. We didn't bring Judi's katanas, after all." He gave the sword a showy twist, then deactivated it and attached it to his belt in one smooth motion. Even though she watched him practice that move on a regular basis, it never failed to impress her.

The crunching of snow made her turn around. She smiled at the deputy who approached. Dressed in head-to-toe snow gear and a bulletproof vest, he nonetheless looked very vulnerable. He pointed to Ted's sword. "You wouldn't happen to have another of those?"

"Oh, no!" Neeta answered for him. "You have a gun. Your job is to keep back and shoot the head."

"Won't the sound attract the others?"

Ted chuckled. "That's Walking Dead. Awesome show, but not accurate. Real zombies don't care one way or another about loud noises, and most will run from gunfire. The habits we have in life are the ones we keep in undeath."

The deputy heaved a sigh. "Good to know. We found the girl. The sheriff's heading that way now. Don't worry—she's trapped. She... You'll see. If you can, try to follow my tracks; we're trying to keep the rest clean so we can figure out where they're headed."

He led them past a white jacket, now marked with a small evidence flag on a spike beside it, and a pinkish-bloodied area that signified a zombie attack. They turned uphill. Now Neeta could hear familiar groaning interspersed with humorless giggling.

"Zombie on drugs," Ted predicted. It wasn't the first time they'd come across someone who had been bitten while high.

They paused at a pit surrounded by rebar and powder-blue caution tape. On it, a big-eyed Earth with cloud arms alternated with the dire warnings not to cross the tape. A little way past, soiled snow told of the reaction by the first deputy to come across the zombie. He now stood back, his pistol out and trained on the creature, while the sheriff looked on. Police tape marked a gore-ridden path from the pit to the attack scene.

Neeta and Ted joined him and looked into the pit. Ted groaned.

The female zombie, young, blonde and newly turned, staggered about the deep hole, bumping into the edges and laughing. It had bites and scratches all up its body, as if something had climbed up it. Its ear had been chewed off, but its face was remarkably intact. A rebar lay beside it, at an angle to the floor. The zombie tripped on it and smashed into the side of the hole, making Rourke jump back. A tunnel opened in the side of the pit, lousy with zombie spoor.

"Had some university folks here yesterday studying the avalanche. Looks like one of our skiers clawed its way out of that hole and got stuck in the pit." The sheriff's voice was detached, professional, but Neeta could hear the undertones of shock.

He twisted to point to some tracks marked by evidence flags. "Looks like Jennifer and Ethan came over, most likely thinking someone needed help. Ethan, for whatever reason, goes to sit over there. Jennifer tries to help the guy out, probably with that rebar, and he attacks her. Pulls her in—or she falls. Can't tell which." Then his voice cracked. "Oh, God! What do I tell Connie and Gunther?"

Neeta set her hand on his shoulder. "Tell them she died trying to help someone." She patted his arm and turned her attention to Ted. "What do you think?"

"I think a pit fight with a corpsicle is a bad idea. Grenade?"

The sheriff drew his sidearm, but he bit back a sob.

"Wait!" Neeta pulled out one of the antihistamine grenades. She whistled to the zombie, who had become fascinated with the blood on the wall and was spreading it like finger paint. Actually, it wasn't a half-bad rendering of the images she'd seen of Arches National Park. A little abstract, maybe…

Neeta whistled again. The zombie turned toward the sound, a raspy groan coming from its open mouth. Neeta lobbed the grenade and hit it in the face.

The canister exploded, coating the undead creature in heavy foam. It reared back, growling, then giggling, clawing at the froth, half-playing with it as the chemicals did their work on its brain. After a few moments of jerking, it slid to the ground and was still. Like so many aspects of zombieism, no one knew why antihistamines worked so well to destroy zombie brain function, but at times like this, Neeta appreciated the gentle approach.

Neeta made a snowball and threw it at the zombie. It bounced off its hair, but the creature did not move. With a nod to Ted, she grabbed a piece of the rebar, walked to the edge closest to the corpsicle's back, and lay down on the snow. Ted grabbed her legs, ready to pull her to safety. She scooched forward until she could reach into the pit. Using the rebar, she pushed the zombie onto its side. She switched on the sword and with a quick, neat, stroke, sliced the back of its neck, severing the spine. She kept her sword activated and trained on the corpsicle until Ted had pulled her back.

"It's safe," Neeta said once she stood, "and at least now, her parents have something to bury."

The deputy turned away to puke again.

"I, uh…" The sheriff stumbled over words—of thanks or chastisement, Neeta couldn't tell, but she didn't give him a chance to clarify.

"So our original undead came out of this hole. Is it safe to guess this is not the one whose arm you found? Okay. One at a time. We know where this one started, and it's left a trail. Looks like it went that way to the boyfriend."

Leaving Buttons to secure the area, Neeta started following the red-flecked tracks, flanked by Ted and a deputy.

"Ethan," Rourke said.

"Ethan—that was the boyfriend? Okay. It took a bite out of Ethan, but he managed to run." She used the rebar to kick up the new snow where it covered the trail. It led to a thicket of trees. There were no clear paths, and already the afternoon sun was casting creepy shadows. Neeta suppressed a shudder.

"You're not going in there?" the deputy asked.

"Listen, um…"

"Benjy."

"Okay, Benjy. If our zombie went this way, there's a chance the trees slowed him down. If so, we can take him out now, before he gets to a populated area. We need to at least try. If you'd rather go back…"

"What? No. I'm okay. I just really don't like the idea of the woods."

She chuckled. "Neither do I. I'm a city girl. But we don't want this corpsicle getting to somewhere that it'll find people."

With Neeta in the lead, Ted in the rear, and a nervous Benjy between them, they tried to follow the broken branches and other signs of the chase. The evergreens cut off most of the light from above, bathing the forest in twilight. Dry branches stuck out at face and chest levels. After Neeta tripped for the second time, snagging but not ripping her suit, she called a halt. "We're not going to find them in here—and it's too easy to get ambushed." She was surprised at how her teeth chattered. Dimly, she heard the beating of helicopter blades.

"Bet that's SLC Z-mat. It'll be dark soon," Benjy agreed. "Maybe they can see something from the air. We should head back to the field, see if we can figure out where the others have gone."

As they retraced their steps, the deputies' walkie-talkies squawked.

"It's a good thing we're heading back. There's a storm coming in fast—the one we expected last night," Benjy told them. "Chopper is searching the area, and said they see skiers matching our zombies upslope—all of them. Looks like they've decided to finish their extreme skiing trip."

"We should go after them," Neeta said.

"Nuh-uh, not with this storm. People die in storms like this."

"Got any sharpshooters in the chopper?" Ted asked as he used his sword to lop off a branch that threatened to pluck at his suit. "Double tap to the brain works as well as a sword."

"I'll ask. They might have time to take a couple out and get to safety before the weather hits."

"Then let's get back fast," Neeta said, and they quickened their pace. Zombies or no, she was going to enjoy a hot bath, warm cocoa, and a roaring fire.

Time enough tomorrow to hunt zombies in the winter wonderland.

While Neeta soaked in her tub with the jets on high and Ted called room service for cocoa and Kahlua, in a snowy ditch not a quarter mile from where they'd turned back, Ethan's corpse blinked in the snow. Slowly, but without difficulty, it sat up, eyes staring ahead like a sleepwalker's. Its mouth moved, trying to form clumsy words, as lungs struggled to remember to breathe. Finally, it spoke.

"Aaaace! Naaachooooes."

It rose, its last thought in life now its first thought in undeath, and made its difficult way downslope to the Ute2 Lodge.

As the storm grew icy, then heavy, then icy again, sleet clung to the shambler, slowing it and covering its features. For a while, the heat of Ethan's suit warded off the cold, but the storm was too much for even its technological prowess. It flashed a recharge warning Ethan no longer had the brain power to heed, then fell dormant. Long after Neeta had gone to bed, dreaming of headless skiers led by a surfing Bergie, the corpse of Ethan Pike succumbed to the cold, muscles freezing in place and stopping even its moaning.

Halfway between the beginner's lift and the lodge, it stood, pointing toward its goal, as the sleet again turned to heavy snow and shrouded the zombie in a thick blanket of white.

Chapter 7

Neeta sped down the hill, her snowboard bumping on the moguls, jarring her knees and her teeth, the cold air biting through the hazmat suit she'd tossed on over pajamas. She kept herself pointed downward and tried to keep her turns tight as possible, but she still could not catch up to the zombie that was chasing a child downslope. Behind her, she heard the roar of an avalanche gaining on her.

If she was going down, she was taking that corpsicle with her! She reached for her belt and grabbed a napalm grenade.

"Whoa! Neeta. That ain't gonna help Global Cooling, you know!"

Beside her, Doug Eidelberg appeared, dressed in board shorts and plastic wrap, ten toes hanging off his surfboard as he rode a wave of snow beside her. One dead arm stretched out past the board, holding his severed head before him, facing Neeta.

"Dudette, we need to talk."

"No!"

Neeta bolted upright in bed, gasping against the urge to scream. She shivered in her silky pajamas; she must have kicked off the covers in her dream. No wonder she was so cold. In her hand, she held, not a napalm grenade, but a small round bottle of Bottum'sUp Rejuv she hadn't drunk last night. She twisted the cap and downed it, then rested her forehead against her knees until her breathing slowed to something resembling normal.

She jumped when Ted knocked on the adjoining door. "Coming!" She swiped her hands over her face, donned her white robe, and went into his room.

He stood by the open sliding door snapping photos. "You gotta see this!"

In the distance toward the lift, kids and a couple of teens were adding snow to a snowman someone must have built the night before. A ski pole hung loosely from its outstretched arm, a Powerbar made a long, flat nose, and a hat with a yarn pom-pom adorned its head.

"Look at the T-shirt!" Ted pointed to the Zombie Death Extreme T-shirt pasted to its body with snowballs.

Neeta leaned against the threshold, admiring. "It's pretty good. You can even see a hint of motion—see how the knee bends? Very natural. Quite a sculpture for snow."

Ted shrugged. "That's nothing. You should see the ice and snow sculptures they do in Canada. Intricate stuff. Still, there is something about this one, isn't there?"

He spun and snapped a photo of her.

"Ted!" She shrieked and shoved her hands in front of his lens. "Delete that, now! What time is it, anyway?"

In answer, her alarm clock started shrieking in the next room.

She sighed. "Playtime's over. Time to get dressed and take out some rotters so we can get back to vacation."

Ted shooed her back to her room, but she heard the click of his camera, followed immediately by "Deleting, promise!" She locked the doors between them, but at least he'd taken her mind off her nightmare.

Unfortunately, another nightmare awaited Neeta at the planning meeting.

"What do you mean, you won't close down the slopes? Your guests aren't safe until we clear out those zombies!" Neeta stepped toward the lodge owner, but Ted grabbed her arm, holding her back. On her other side, Deputy Benjy, whom the sheriff had put in charge of the zombie problem, stepped closer, though he did not touch her.

The lodge owner, Altimeter Brown, a slick black man in designer turtleneck and jeans, spread his hands. Behind him, the lodge manager stood, looking small and helpless. "I have absolutely no proof that they're any threat to my business."

"Your business?"

"Calm yourself, Ms. Lyffe. SLC Z-Mat said they were skiing miles from here. In fact, their captain is prepping the helicopter to go check on them as we speak."

"You mean he hasn't checked yet? Yes, they were on the mountain. Ten hours ago. They could have made their way here by now—and you've started the lifts without anyone securing the slopes!"

How could this guy be so oblivious? No, so calm. Neeta wanted to squeeze that calm right out of his eyeballs. Beside her, Ted must have noticed because he put his hand on the small of her back. It might have looked like a gesture of support, but she knew it was so he could grab her sweater if she got the urge to leap across the desk at oh-so-calm Brown.

"I called in all our ski patrol personnel. They're monitoring the slopes."

Oh, it gets better! Civilians out on the slope thinking they're authorities. Calm, Neeta. Calm. "What have you trained them to do about zombies?"

Benjy cleared his throat. "They were told to keep an eye out and report. We'll shut down lifts if anyone sees anything suspicious."

"There, you see?" Brown crossed his arms. "We've got it under control. After all, you don't want to ruin these poor people's vacations, do you?"

"I think they'll consider it a lot more ruined if someone dies." When he merely shrugged, she snarled. She'd thought the director of Zombie Death Extreme had been obstinate. With the deputy present, she couldn't threaten Brown with a chainsaw like she had Dave, either. She looked to Ted for support, but all he offered was a shrug.

"Fine! Then I want free rein of this lodge and all its facilities. If Ted or I need to get somewhere to take out some corpsicle having a vacation on your slopes, I do not want to wait more than a second before a snowmobile, a lift, or whatever is taking us to it. If I say clear an area, it gets cleared immediately. I want your lodge employees armed with bottles of bleach, and I want to talk to all of them about the best things to do if a zombie is sighted indoors."

Brown smiled at her as if he found her cute and amusing. "Shouldn't you be out there finding the—what did you call them? Corpsicles?—before they get into my lodge? I know my exterminator is able to keep the vermin outside."

Before Neeta could strike out, physically or verbally, Ted stepped between them. "Boss, why don't you go meet the SLC Z-mat guys and come up with a plan of action, and I'll get Manager Witherspoon here to call together all the employees for a crash course on zombie basics?"

Neeta pushed past Ted and pinned Altimeter Brown with her glare. "If anyone gets hurt by a zombie, I swear I will cut off its arm and use it to smack some sense into you." With a nod of dismissal to Ted, she spun and swept from the room, Benjy in tow. The door closed as Brown said something about his mother-in-law being right.

"Lamebrain," Neeta muttered, figuring the deputy would think she was talking about the zombie rather than Brown, but not really caring either way. Why was it her fate to get the stupid customers? "Okay, Benjy. Where's the Z-Mat team?" she asked.

Benjy looked pale but impressed. "You'd really smack him with a zombie's arm?"

"Yes!" She took a calming breath. "I'd wrap it first. No one deserves to be infected. Let's get these undead before they infect anyone themselves. Z-Mat?"

"They're prepping the helicopter. The wind was too wild earlier or they'd have already gone. They're taking up a sharpshooter from the Ogden SWAT team. Figured the best bet is double-tap, like Ted suggested. They tried yesterday, but didn't have any luck. Problem is, the zombies are fast; between their gnarly skills and the motion of the chopper, the Z-Mat shooters couldn't get a bead."

Neeta exited the lodge, but paused on the porch, thinking. She'd never gotten to use guns. California had banned all firearms in the Guns Do 2 Kill Act of 2025. Now only criminals were lucky enough to defend themselves that way against the undead, although most were too stupid or freaked to aim for the head. Not a problem here, however. If only they could get the zombies to slow down…

Skiers were already out in force: kids headed for bunny slopes, older teens giggling and wrestling as they crunched through snow toward more thrilling runs, adults of all ages and skill levels. She longed to shout out a warning, but without any plan of action, she'd probably only start a panic. Besides, she wouldn't put it past Altimeter Brown to sue her for loss of business. She had enough trouble balancing her mortgage against her other stupid, expensive lawsuit.

But they were so innocent, building snowmen, learning to ski, taking photos. She watched as some skiers paused to mug it up for a news team getting footage of the pre-race activities.

Suddenly, she grinned and did a sharp rear march back to the lodge, pulling her cell phone out of her pocket. "Ted, did you bring your big camera—the professional one? Awesome. I have a plan."

✗

"See, babe? Interesting! I mean, when else would I have a chance to film while hanging out of a helicopter?"

Ted leaned out the helicopter's door, to be grabbed by the two Z-Mat officers securing his rigging. He already had his camera tied to himself with a safety line.

Neeta crossed her arms and regarded her fiancé with mixed feelings. She loved how he could make lemonade out of the lemon their vacation had become; yet his risk-taking gave her unpleasant butterflies in her stomach. The peaceful mountain view of the lodge's heliport didn't offer any comfort.

"Just don't take any chances. You're there to distract the zombies, not to record."

"Yeah, but if I do get some good digital, we are so selling it to the news! We'll offer it to Extreme Sports first."

"That's fair. They are your disguise."

On the tail of the chopper, four members of the Z-mat team were covering the police markings with banners that advertised the channel's sponsorship and coverage of the event. Neeta had used her agreement with Brown to commandeer them. She didn't know how the ski team had felt about the authorities in life, but if the current competitors were any indication, they'd be glad to pose for the camera, offering the SWAT sharpshooter a chance to take them out easy.

The officers working on Ted declared themselves satisfied and smacked him on the back.

Attached to the pulley but not the second belt that would secure him to the helicopter's floor, Ted hopped out, trailing cable to where Neeta stood. He wore his ski clothes, and a headset replaced his helmet. She didn't like it. She wanted him in a nice, safe hazmat suit, but if he didn't play the part of a cameraman, the ruse might not work. Ted put his arms around her. "You're the one that needs to be careful, wandering through those woods looking for ARMs on foot. Will you take the chainsaw?"

She shook her head. "It's too close quarters. I'm more likely to get it caught in a tree."

He held out his sword. "Take Enigo. I can't use it in the chopper, anyway."

She hated the idea of him being disarmed, but he had already slapped his sword into her hand. He loved that thing. It was named for a Guatemalan exterminator, but she knew his big hope was to go against a six-fingered zombie someday. She attached the sword to her belt. He wouldn't take no for an answer, and he did have a point. Besides, she kind of liked it when he got all protective.

"Just don't fall out. I don't care how good you are at it."

His expression grew thoughtful. "I've never jumped out of a helicopter before…"

Before he could finish his thought, she grabbed him by the lapels and kissed him. He stiffened in surprise, then wrapped his arms around her and returned the kiss until the Z-Mat team got tired of waiting and reeled him into the chopper. She stepped back as the rotors started. When he started filming her, she waved until the helicopter had pointed itself toward the avalanche zone.

He was probably safer in the air than she was on the ground…if he didn't decide to jump out the helicopter, of course. That didn't keep her from worrying. She turned back to the parking lot, making herself turn her mind to her own part of the job, and nearly ran into a woman standing right in her path.

"Well, Neeta Lyffe. I am disappointed."

"Mandy Culver?" Neeta gaped. She still recognized that lush blonde hair and the perfect turned-up nose, even though it had been over a decade since they'd last seen each other. Mandy had treated Neeta to such a miserable weekend that she still ranked in Neeta's private list of people she'd like to see die, then come back as zombies so she could rekill them.

Sadly, Mandy was very much alive, and just as gorgeous and well dressed as she'd been as an adolescent. She also still had that tilt to her head that said, "I had a Daddy, so I'm better than you."

Despite her inner 12-year-old's sudden urge to come out with a screech and bared nails, Neeta pasted on a professional smile. "Well. Mandy. This…is a surprise."

"I'm Amanda Brown now, and is it, really?"

Of course it was, but as usual, Amanda seemed to know more than Neeta. "Oh! So, you married Altimeter Brown?"

"He prefers 'Tim,' and obviously, I have." She looked pointedly at Neeta's bare hands. "I see you haven't been able to make a similar commitment yet."

Neeta almost protested she was engaged, but her ring was in the room safe and they still hadn't settled on a date. It wasn't this woman's business, anyway. Why was she letting this childhood annoyance waylay her when there were corpsicles on skis to worry about? "If you'll excuse me, I'm rather busy at the moment."

"You should be busy promoting this event." Her bossy, know-it-all tone made Neeta wish again for claws. "We took a chance with you, you know. Despite our past, I told Tim you should do this event. I extended the olive branch of Christian peace and charity—and instead of accepting it, you try to close down the competition and then steal banners?"

Neeta crossed her arms to hide how her hands had curled into fists. She was trying to save lives that this woman's husband only saw as profits—and Mandy was going to waste her time accusing her of theft? "I didn't steal them; I borrowed them, with purpose. You do realize there are zombies on the loose?"

Mandy tossed her head; her hair, which stuck out from her hat in perfect curls, flounced. Neeta wondered how long she'd spent primping in front of the mirror wearing the hat to get that effect. "They're in the hills, Neeta, miles away."

She found herself mimicking Mandy's exasperated tone. "They're not like coyotes or bears, Mandy. They will go after humans, kill and infect them if given a chance, a hundred percent guaranteed. Plus, they're on skis."

Mandy held up a hand in front of her face, dismissing Neeta's words. "I thought Operation Homefront was something we had in common. I know Dad chose me…"

Even a decade and more later, Neeta still didn't know what that meant. "Look, I came here to promote this contest and to snowboard with my fiancé. I didn't ask for your zombies to interfere with my working vacation, but since they are here, and since I've been asked for my expertise, I'll do my best to get rid of your little infestation so that you can go on with your contest, and I can get back to my fun."

She walked past, just avoiding brushing Mandy with her shoulder. When she was 12, they'd been fairly even in size, but now, Neeta knew she could easily knock Amanda Brown over if she wanted to. Because she wanted to, she was careful not to. She still shuddered remembering when she lost her temper and went after Marcel Chelemas with an activated sword.

"Neeta!" Mandy called after her. "I forgive you! You are my sister, and I love you in the name of Jesus."

Neeta raised a hand in both acknowledgement and dismissal but didn't turn around as she headed to the snowmobile. She had things to rekill.

The ocean had indeed totaled her fancy helmet, and the new one was on order, but her old one still worked fine and had a passable Bluetooth that connected to her phone. Even with the roar of the snowmobile, she could still hear the splashing of a swimming pool and the squeals of kids in the background at her friend Min's house in Malibu. Meanwhile, a chilly wind blew snow sideways at her as she headed up the mountain. The warm sounds of a California winter made her feel colder still—or would have if she still hadn't been so hot about Mandy.

"That's so quaked," Min said in that careful voice that said she was holding back full judgment until she got all the facts. "I remember how your mom made you play with her that whole weekend. 'Course, that was right after Dad died, so I wasn't up for playing, anyway."

"I'd have rather been with you." Jerry Lee was Neeta's mom's business partner and the closest thing to a father Neeta had had. He'd died on an extermination job gone bad. "I didn't want to play, either."

"Yeah. So, she got you this gig?"

"She approved me for this appearance or suggested me or something, she said," Neeta corrected. "HumVans arranged it—and to hear her talk, I personally resurrected those skiers from the dead just to ruin her husband's contest."

"Resurrected? That's an interesting choice of words. Hey, I'm Googling her now."

"Oh, you should have heard her: 'Jesus has commanded me to love you!' I mean, am I that hard to love?"

"How come you're not talking to Ted about this?"

"I tried, but he's in a helicopter, hoping to take out some zombies from the air. He could hardly hear me, and all I could hear was whuppa-whuppa-whuppa."

"Well, helicopter blades are loud." She paused to yell something at her youngest.

"No, that was Ted." She imitated his voice. "'I can't hear you, babe; I'm in a helicopter! Whuppa-whuppa-whuppa.' How'd I fall for such a clown?"

"You need the laughter in your life. Found her! Amanda Brown, wife of Altimeter Brown. Oh, get this—she's clergy!"

"What?" In her surprise, Neeta gunned the engine. The snowmobile hit a bump in the road that sent her airborne for just a minute. She gave an involuntary shriek.

"No, seriously! Parson Amanda Brown of the New Fellowship of Christ Parish. So she was dead serious when she said she loved you in the name of Christ. That's kind of cool, actually. She was such a troll when we were kids."

"I guess. Glad I kept my temper. Hey, I'm coming to my stop. I'll talk to you later."

"Okay—and Neeta? Do be careful, because I really do love you like my sister, and I don't want anything to happen to you."

"Don't worry! I'm not dying until I'm legally Mrs. Neeta Lyffe-Hacker, and all our kids are grown and maybe married to each other. Oh, I didn't even tell you about what Mandy said about that. Never mind; I'll call you when I get done and we can snark about Parson Brown some more, okay?"

Still, Neeta swallowed down a lump in her throat as she pulled up beside the snowmobile of the Z-Mat officer she'd be working with. She should have known better than to call Min before going after the undead.

Chapter 8

Neeta paused on the seat of her snowmobile and took a slow breath, trying unsuccessfully to clear her mind of guilt. What had she been thinking, calling Min right before an extermination? Uncle Jerry had died on the job, bitten by a zombie, then returned four months later to terrorize his family. Min had cried every time she knew Neeta's mom was going after the undead—and now, she was probably crying again.

And praying. Min always prays. Neeta scanned the snow-laden forest, trying to see through the trees for any sign of a zombie, but all she saw were dark trunks, like sentinels, protecting anything that might be shambling within. I'm a city girl. Even in the parks, we try to flush them out. Maybe it was a good thing I called. I'll need Min's prayers.

"Ms. Lyffe?"

Neeta blinked away her dark thoughts and turned to the officer who had pulled up behind her.

The SLC Z-Mat officer wore a thick HazMat suit with SCAM stenciled over the pocket. She had a rifle with a powerful targeting scope in her hand and a pistol holstered in the belt of her suit. Neeta hadn't seen many guns in her life, but she was pretty sure most didn't have a barrel that big. Did it work in close quarters, though?

The woman held out her hand.

"I'm Brooklyn Bridges—hence, the nickname." She motioned at the pocket. "Call me 'Brook.' It's an honor to be working with you—and a little bit of a relief, to be frank. The only experience I've had with actual undead has been under controlled conditions—but we do train! Hard," she added hastily.

Neeta put on her most confident smile and shook the woman's hand. "Nice to meet you, Brook. Did you train in the woods? Good, because

I'm used to back alleys and warehouses. You do have more than just the guns, right?"

Brook released Neeta's hand and turned hers over so Neeta could see the tubing and nozzle strapped to her wrist. "Antifreeze. We find it works just about as well as bleach. In the pockets, I have some ski magazines, cans of Bottum'sUp Extreme, and a couple of joints, just in case we run into Ethan, and…" With some pride, she pulled out a large ax. "I know, I know, but my parents were big Walking Dead fans and as a woman in this line of work, I felt I needed something more—I don't know—tough, I guess. Besides, I like the heft of it when I swing it around."

Neeta nodded, impressed. "I feel the same way about chainsaws. We're going to get along just fine."

Brook returned her ax to its back sheath with a practiced motion, then pulled something else off her belt and strapped it to her wrist. "Motion detector and GPS. Limited range, but it should give us some warning. We're here." She pointed to two yellow blips and traced her finger along the map. "Here is where you had to call off the search yesterday because of the storm. There's another one on the way, incidentally. The wind gusts are giving the chopper a hard time. On the bright side, they had to shut down some of the upper lifts at the resort. Oh, and your partner said he's getting a lot of awesome recordings of extreme zombie skiing."

"Fuze core." Neeta dismounted and loaded herself up with her own arsenal. Together, they headed into the woods.

* * * * * * * * * * *

Ted leaned slightly out over the helicopter and laughed. They'd attached a short cable to him to connect him to one side of the chopper so that he didn't sway too much and get in the sharpshooter's way. "I love my job! Turbulence is awesome."

Despite the thumping of the rotors, he heard someone mutter, "Maniac," over the headset before the sharpshooter spoke. "Well, I for one am glad it's over. No way was I going to line up a headshot with all that bouncing around."

"If anyone can do this, it's you," the pilot cut in. "Looks like luck favors us now, though. Wind's dying down. We can make a couple of runs, get their attention, then go for the rekill—but you'll need to be fast."

"Fast is my middle name." Nonetheless, he took his time hefting himself out of his seat and lying on the floor of the chopper. Tall as well as portly, he took up a lot of the floor. Ted scooted to give him some room. The others strapped him down as he got his rifle into position. Ted did not envy him; his feet were already getting numb from the cold and the vibration.

"Stay out of my line of fire," he warned Ted. "Even with nanotechnology assisting the targeting, this is not going to be easy. I need to get a good steady lock, and you need to be out of the way."

"Roger," Ted replied, his voice firm and serious as his mind turned to business.

As soon as they got close to the zombies, however, Ted whooped and hollered out, "Yeah! Show me what you've got!" as he panned the area with his camera. Again, he heard someone mutter, "Maniac," over the headset, and he laughed.

Below, the zombies responded as any publicity-loving extreme sportsman might. Two put on more speed; a third chose to do some showy dynamic turns that sprayed a cloud of powder that obscured it. One used an ice-covered ravine as a half-pipe, and the one that had been carrying its board back up the hill jumped on and sped down before their shooter could get a lock. He swore and called another target.

The boarding zombie with a missing arm took a natural ramp. If flipped in the air, its board describing a perfect circle around its still head. Suddenly, its skull exploded and it flopped awkwardly to the ground.

"Gotcha! Line me another!"

"Can you get lower and in front of them?" Ted asked the pilot. "Maybe they'll stay still for a smile-and-wave."

The chopper swooped ahead of two skiers that had decided to show their skills by skiing together to trace a neat double-helix of tracks in the snow. As it lowered to a hover, the skiers made a synchronized stop and indeed raised their hands in a wave.

"Yeah, smile for the camera," the sharpshooter muttered.

Before he could fire, however, one of the zombies jerked and fell, its back bloody with shotgun holes. The other zombie shrieked and sped off as a second gunshot kicked up snow in its wake.

"Double tap!" Ted yelled, but it was too late. The helicopter pilot had jerked the stick in surprise. By the time he got them righted, the wounded zombie had disappeared.

"Where are they?" Ted called to the others. "Maybe we can distract them."

"Too late!" One of the team on the other side pointed and Ted saw tracks that disappeared into the woods. A little farther down, he saw two snowmobiles.

Swearing the Korean profanities Neeta had taught him, he fumbled with his phone to call her.

Despite her earlier misgivings about the forest, instincts took over as Neeta made her stealthy way down the narrow trail. It was actually a little easier than tracking a zombie in a warehouse. Very few undead climbed trees, not that she thought the thin and winter-dry branches would bear the weight if any tried. Thus, she only needed to concern herself with one level, whereas in a warehouse, she'd have to keep checking the walkways above and below. Plus the snow made a soft crunching under their boots. With only the occasional plop of snow falling from a heavy-laden branch, they would be able to hear a zombie coming from way off—if Brook stopped talking.

"Still no motion...except for that doe we passed. Wasn't she beautiful? Bet there's a herd nearby. So have you and Ted set a date yet? It's just, we're all big fans of Zombie Death Extreme back in Salt Lake. How come you're not hosting anymore?"

"I didn't want to leave LA. I have clients." Neeta had taken the lead and had found broken branches and torn clothing that told of someone's hasty escape and another's pursuit. If only the snow hadn't covered the footprints.

"Wow. People really hire you to exterminate zombies?" Neeta heard her shuffling as she did a sweep behind them. Brook might babble, but she did know her job.

"It's an option in my contract. Mostly, I take care of ants, termites, the usual."

Brook snorted. "You make it sound pedantic."

"I wish." Her phone sang out with Ted's ringtone. She answered, "Whuppa-whuppa-whuppa."

"Get off the trail!" Ted's voice held no humor. "Some idiot with a shotgun spooked the corpsicles."

"Neeta…" Uncertainty made Brook drag out the name. "I have motion…"

"Babe, they're in the forest, heading your way!"

"Neeta! Lots of motion, coming this way, fast!"

"It's them. Back against a tree!" Without bothering to hang up, she shoved her phone back into her pocket. Out of habit, she traced a line in the trail in front of herself with her squirt gun as she put her back to a tree. Brook did the same without being told and tossed a magazine and couple of unopened cans of energy drink on the trail for good measure. Neeta's confidence rose. Brook was sharp and well trained.

Neeta pulled out her sword and faced the trail. If the zombies were coming the way they had, and on skis, they might be able to take them out as it passed.

On the opposite side of the trail, Brook had picked up her intention fast and held her ax drawn and ready. Already they heard the rustle of trees and the frantic plop-plop-plop of snow being shaken from branches. A pounding thunder grew louder. That couldn't be the zombies, so what…?

Small white mounds bounded toward them, and then a couple dozen snow bunnies brushed past, scattering her protective circle and shredding the magazine. A small fox overtook the rabbits, interested only in escape. It ran right over her boot, distracting her momentarily from the fast-approaching deer.

"Moose!" Brook yelled.

The two flung themselves off the trail as the huge, terrified creature galloped past, its antlers narrowly missing Neeta's helmet.

Swish! In its wake, a zombie skied past so fast that, by the time Neeta re-activated her sword, it was out of her range.

With a grunt of effort, Brook threw her ax.

It caught the zombie squarely in the back, surprising it enough that it ran head first into a tree. Its arms and legs flung out before it, and it slid down the trunk to a sitting position. There it stayed, moaning, "Loser."

The thunder settled back to quiet but for the zombie groaning into the tree trunk.

"That looks familiar." Neeta walked up to the corpsicle and removed its head with a clean slice. With one foot against the corpse's back she grabbed the ax handle and pulled it out, presenting the gory thing to Brook. "Good work, Brook.

Come on; call in this location, then let's see if we can catch another one."

"I did it," Brook whispered, then squealed and did a little dance in the stampede-trodden trail. "I did it! I rekilled a zombie—with Neeta Lyffe!"

After Brook's thrilling first rekill, they had no luck at all finding any traces of the other zombies. They'd backtracked the trail in hopes of discovering ski tracks or some spoor from the one who had been shot, but all they found was snowy dirt churned up by the fleeing animals. With a new storm moving in, they decided to bag the zombies they'd killed, along with as much of the contaminated snow and debris they could. It was a long haul to get the bags to the helicopter, which met them at the clearing.

The chopper had landed, and a portable decontamination tent had been set up. Neeta heard a whimper escape her throat when she saw it. This was going to be so cold.

Brook must have been reading her mind. "At least it wasn't too messy. The decontam spray is fast, too. We figured if anything would happen,

Murphy's Law would require it to be in the middle of winter."

Ted was waiting outside the tent. His stomach looked twice its normal size.

"I've got your clothes under my coat to warm them up," he said as she got near and pointed.

Brook put her hand on her heart and cooed.

"I can put yours on the engine block," one of her fellow officers teased, but she heartily agreed.

A few frigid minutes later, they were clean and dressed, and the helicopter was on its way with the remains to a biohazard handling facility. Neeta let Ted drive the snowmobile, but even snuggled against his back, she was freezing by the time they returned.

Neeta trudged into the lodge, her mind on a long hot soak and dinner in her room with a fire burning, wrapped up in warm blankets—and maybe snuggling Ted, if she could keep her eyes open. Usually, she had a rush after taking out the undead, but today, she just wanted to lie down and sleep. Who knew cold could be so exhausting?

Naturally, she entered her room to find an urgent request from the contest organizer, Eric Peterson. The lodge's dining/shopping area was full of skiers stuck indoors from the storm, and would she please, please, please spend an hour or two at a table he'd arranged on the dining level, signing autographs and talking up the contest and Operation Homefront? She moaned.

Ted kissed her head. "A hot shower will help, and I'll bring a big pot of coffee to your table."

She leaned against his chest. "All right, but only for an hour or so. I'm starving. I want hot soup, followed by a hot entrée, with hot tea and hot chocolate for dessert. I may never be warm again!"

He squeezed her closer. "I'll bring our tablets down, too, and we can discuss a wedding date. That'll warm you up."

The shower took the edge off the cold, but she still dressed in layers, topped with the bulky sweater Ted had bought her their first night there. She went to the table feeling like a potato. Ted brought her a pot of coffee as promised, and then left to wander the hallways with brochures that boasted HumVan's support of Operation Homefront. On the first page of the slick trifold brochure bore a photo of Neeta posing in front of her custom HumVan while holding a photo of her mom. The interior pages explained the charity and had testimonies and donation instructions. He directed people to the table, where she signed autographs and told stories the charity had given her about folks they'd helped in Utah, as well as how they had helped her mother with two years' interest-free mortgage.

Fifty minutes later, when the coffee was burning a hole in her empty stomach rather than warming her and the flow of autograph-seekers had slowed to less than a trickle, Ted returned to the table. He held their tablets in one hand and gestured at her in courtly fashion with the other. "My lady, our reservation is in five minutes."

She half-expected him to lead her to the snack bar, High Snackage, which was stationed beside the cannabis boutique – handcrafted joints for every occasion! The little eatery obviously catered to the same clientele. Even though neither of them partook, Neeta and Ted had spent a good five minutes laughing over the menu in the window. They'd wanted to try it for lunch after a hard morning's skiing, but the zombies had ruined that idea.

Instead, however, Ted led her to the swankier restaurant on the top floor. With its quiet music, subdued lighting and sophisticated décor, it obviously catered to a different clientele than High Snackage. She gave Ted a smile of gratitude and squeezed his hand.

The hostess led them to a back booth where they could talk without being overheard. They sat side by side so they could look at their Slates together over a pot of herbal tea. Ted snuggled in closer, setting his chin on her shoulder as she called up a color-coded calendar.

"This isn't going to be easy," Ted said.

"Nothing in my life is—nothing worthwhile, anyway." In addition to their work schedule and their friends' special occasions, she'd put in the dates of important political rallies and primaries for California and the neighboring states—high risk times for zombie sightings. Ted had added the calendars of his mom and many "cousins" as well as big music concerts and special events within a 50-mile radius of Inglewood that might also attract the undead. Somewhere in there, they needed to find two free weeks for a wedding and honeymoon.

Neeta leaned back to give him a quick kiss. "We don't leave here tonight without a plan." They bumped fists on it.

Altimeter Brown walked to their table and peered down at them. Mandy stood beside him, her arm tucked into his. They dressed in matching turtlenecks and jeans. "I hope those are battle plans to protect my resort."

"Wedding plans, actually," Neeta said with a smile and her most closed voice. "We'd appre -"

"Wedding!" Mandy exclaimed and slid into the booth seat opposite them. "So you were kissing your fiancé at the helicopter? I'm so embarrassed, after the comment I made earlier."

"Which comment?" The words were out of her mouth before she realized she was speaking them. Naturally, Altimeter took that as permission to join them. Neeta kicked herself. In the corner of her eye, she saw Ted watching Mandy with puzzled intensity. What did he see?

Mandy set her hands on the table entreatingly. "The comment about you having commitment issues. I just assumed, given your family background…"

Ted typed something one handed on her pad. Rabid fan?

Neeta replied with a shrug emoticon.

Ted leaned forward and held out his hand. "Ted Hacker—Neeta's fiancé. You are…?"

Mandy smiled and introduced herself as Parson Amanda Brown. "But I'm sure Neeta's told you about me." Her smile faded as she took in Ted's apologetic look and Neeta's confused one. "No? I thought… I mean, I told Tim everything about us."

"Us? What 'us'?" Again, the words slipped from her mouth. Maybe this woman was crazy.

"Hey, you guys have the same scowl brow," Ted said.

Mandy sat back, hands up in surrender. "No, it's fine. I just thought, you know, with Dad gone, that as sisters, we could…"

Neeta had chainsawed her way through hoards of zombies that were less oppressive than this woman's attempt to guilt her, and she was not going to give in to her manipulations now. She leaned forward on her elbows, pushing her cup of tea to the side. "Listen, I'm sorry for your loss, but that does not make us sisters."

"Uh, babe…"

She glanced at Altimeter and Ted, including them in the conversation. "Look, Mandy. The only time we met was when I was twelve years old. Your mother showed up at our door, and she and Mom argued for two days straight. I was assigned to entertain you, but all you did was go on and on about how your daddy loved you and chose you. Which, you know, good for you, but I still don't get why you rubbed my nose in it. That's all the contact we've ever had. You're not a sister. You're not a friend. You're barely an acquaintance. So if you don't mind…"

"She never told you." Mandy's jaw dropped open and she covered it with one hand before speaking again. "I can't believe she never told you."

This time, Neeta clamped her mouth shut before she got dragged into more drama. Ted, however, leaned forward and also spoke softly. "Neeta doesn't know anything about her birth father."

Neeta rested her head in one hand and tried to rub away her scowl brow. What had happened to the romantic dinner while picking a wedding date? At least she wasn't cold anymore. "So?"

"Babe, I don't think the parson means you're her sister 'in Christ.'"

Neeta peeked under her hand at Ted, then Mandy. Mandy had turned her face toward the wall as she wiped a tear from her cheek.

"Your mother never said anything?" she asked in a small voice.

Mandy? My sister? Meaning her dad… Neeta dropped her hand slowly. "She told me. She was in the Marines. She had a one-night lapse in judgment. They both knew it was a bad idea. She didn't even know she was pregnant until she got injured. She fell in love with Duncan McCain, the physical therapist who helped her learn to use her new arm. He would have been my dad, but he got deployed and was killed before I was born. She decided to accept an honorable discharge on disability, bought the house in Inglewood and started a new life. As far as I know, she never thought of my biodad after that one night."

Mandy shook her head, mouth twisted in an expression of pity. "My mom told me everything—she always believed in honesty, especially after what Dad did. Your mom got the house with the help of Operation Homefront because Dad recommended her for it—and he gave her $25,000 to get herself started. He never told Mom about any of it, until she found files on his computer of you with your mom—public appearances for zombie laws, lobbies, articles... You winning some school award. So she confronted him. She made him delete everything, and then confess to us all and reassure us that he loved us and chose us over you. Then, she went to California to get back the money he had given your mother."

Mandy suddenly leaned forward, almost pleading. "She didn't want anything to tie him to her or you. You have to understand; her marriage was in peril."

"What money?" Even as she said it, she realized. Her mother had told her stories of how, when she was recovering from her last surgery and was coherent enough to be wondering how she was going to forge a future, she'd been looking at her online account and found a deposit of $25,000. No record of who sent it to her; just a thank you note. She'd always thought it was the family of someone she'd saved the day she lost her arm.

So, her Mom didn't know the truth until Mandy's mother pounded on their door demanding it back. She closed her eyes, remembering: Her mother telling the woman she was crazy until she said some man's name. She'd turned to Neeta, and her face had been so pale, Neeta didn't even argue when she told her to go play outside with the woman's daughter.

Mandy was still deep into her confession. "All that money we took from you, and we just wasted it. It's not like we were destitute. Mom said we needed to 'reunite as a family.' We spent two weeks in Florida that year, took a Disney cruise... It wasn't until I found Christ that I gave any thought to how we must have impoverished your family. It's plagued me, which is why when we had the chance to hire you..."

So we were a pity hire? Somehow, that hit Neeta harder than this strange news about a biodad she never thought about. Neeta's hands curled into fists. She forced them to relax. She had a wedding date to set and zombies to decapitate, and she wasn't going to get either done if her newfound half-sister kept showing up with her passive-aggressive guilt trip and romanticized version of Poor Orphan Neeta.

"Let me put you at ease. My mom never told me who you were or why you visited. I'm going to take a guess it's because your mom didn't want me busting in on your family's unity, and that was just fine by mine. Your dad was never a part of my life."

"But your mom must have said something! I mean, we both have Dad's eyes."

Neeta pressed her fingers to her temples, hiding her eyes. What was Mandy told?

Under the table, Ted squeezed her knee. She didn't know if he was trying to reassure her or just remind her of his presence.

She should probably pick her words carefully, but she was never good at tact. Besides, it's not like there was a Dear Zoe guide for this...or was there?

"Mandy, Mom was on leave after some heavy battles. She got drunk and had a one-night stand. I don't think there was any romantic eye-gazing. I'm not even sure she looked at his eyes long enough to know what color they were. She was stupid—her words.

"She never would have made your dad choose between her and your mom. There were no ties. She wasn't interested in your—our—father. She never contacted him. As for the money—she never knew who gave it to her. She got an anonymous transfer into her Bitcoin account with the note,

'Thank you for your sacrifice.' She always thought that meant on the battlefield. I know because she had a screenshot of it with her military citations.

"She did take out a second mortgage that year. I guess she paid your mom. I never knew what it was about, and I never asked. I figured it was for the business. She bought some new equipment, expanded her advertising, and got me my first surfboard so I could take lessons with my best friend. If it weren't for that stupid lawsuit I've been slapped with, I'd have paid off the house by now. So you can put any guilty fantasies you have of us eating out of garbage cans and wearing rags out of your mind."

"Surely, you must have wondered, especially now, getting married?" Mandy's earnestness only made Neeta more obstinate.

"No, I did not. I had my mom. Uncle Jerry, her business partner, was a father to me. Incidentally..."

She shut her mouth on her words. Mandy's mother had stormed their door the morning after her Uncle Jerry's funeral, only minutes before they were going to Min's house. So instead of grieving with her best friend, she'd put up with Mandy all weekend. Still, that wasn't Mandy's fault, and there wasn't any sense nuking her about it. That was a long time in the past, and if she wanted Mandy to let go, she needed to, as well.

Still, she wasn't done being angry about the present. "As far as hiring us—we came here at the invitation of the contest organizers and the request of HumVans. It's in my contract, and I'm glad to help the charity. Plus, we thought it would be a nice place to relax and make some wedding plans. After all, Utah doesn't have zombies, right?"

She threw up her hands and barely missed whacking her fiancé on the nose. "But, now that you have an infestation, Ted and I are offering our expertise, for which we will bill you our standard rate, and which services you have the option to refuse. SLC Z-Mat is here, after all. We can deal with your zombies, but I will not deal with your personal family issues. If that's why we were brought here, pay us for our work so far, and we'll be gone tomorrow, HumVans be damned."

She gave Ted a tight smile. "How about Phoenix, babe? It's warm in Phoenix, right?"

His fingers played on his tablet. "Eighty-two tomorrow! Some great galleries, too, plus a They Mite B Robots concert day after tomorrow."

She pinned Altimeter with a challenging glare. His lodge; his decision. She didn't care if Mandy gave her "permission" or not.

Altimeter leaned back with a sigh. After a moment, he asked, "Are they on my resort?"

"We're not sure," Ted answered. "That hunter spooked them, but they probably have enough brains to take shelter from the storm. Either way, it will slow them down.. We're meeting with Z-Mat tomorrow morning."

Altimeter regarded his wife, who sat, quiet and ashen-faced, her eyes downcast. When she did not move, he asked Neeta, "Can you handle this discreetly?"

"That depends on the corpsicles," Neeta replied, "but we have years of experience dealing with undead in everything from concerts to voting booths."

"We've already got contracts to keep the dead from voting in four California state primaries," Ted added, "and from attending the Grateful Dead Two concert in LA. Gotta love the irony."

"Which is why we're trying to find a time next year to get married. I see. Well, then, if you'll excuse us…"

Altimeter cleared his throat and tapped his still-dazed wife on the hand. She jerked and followed him out of the seat, giving Neeta one indecipherable look as they left.

Neeta sighed and flopped back, resting her head against the seatback.

"That was intense," Ted opined.

She shut her eyes. "Let's think about it after we set a date and take out some corpsicles."

"You're so hot when you talk about marriage and rekilling," he kidded, then his voice gentled. "You all right?"

She did an internal inventory and found that she was. Okay, discovering that #8 on her People I Wish I Could Rekill list was her half-sister would take some processing, and they had a half-dozen zombies to worry about, but otherwise she felt fine. Maybe even better than when she'd first sat down at the table. Finally, the adrenalin spike she'd hoped for!

No, if Mandy expected her to feel loss over a man she never knew, she was going to be disappointed. There had been fathers in her life—Uncle Jerry, and then Jason Hollerman. In fact, Jason had already told her he was walking her down the aisle when she married Ted.

Ted. Now there was Dad material! She grinned at her fiancé, warming as his face mirrored her expression. Behind him, the waitress cleared her throat. She held two soup bowls in her hands. Apparently, she'd been waiting to serve them for a while. "So…are we ready?"

"You know what?" Neeta told her. "I think we'd like to get those to take up to my room."

High Snackage Menu

Welcome to High Snackage! It's our mission to proactively synergize with the marijuana-fueled palate to provide our customers a value-added experience with the unlikeliest of tasty treats – and if you're clean, have we got a culinary adventure for you! Check out these awesome entrees. If you don't find them Aces, we'll get you another snack free.

Haggis ice cream: Protein and cream, made from sheep lovingly cared for by students at BYU and Utah State. Rated the #1 treat for the Baked of London, you won't find anything baaaad about this!

Flavored Cheezees: So cheesy! So crunchy! That funny feeling you get on the roof of your mouth after eating a bag. What's there not to love about this multi-sensual culinary experience? Well, we've taken them to the next level with these added flavorings:

➢ **Bacon!** Because…bacon!

➢ **Burrito.** As long as you're trippin', head south of the border with this awesome addition. Comes in chicken or beef. Extra cilantro on request.

➢ **Vanilla Bean.** You can't go wrong with vanilla.

➢ **Java.** This isn't just flavoring, mind you. We've pulverized roasted Columbian expresso beans into a fine powder. Get a caffeine jolt to juice your mellow.

Whipped cream sliders. Freshly made yeast rolls stuffed with ReadyWhip. It's like a donut sandwich. In fact, if you need something more substantial, we'll add spray bacon and spray cheese. Dinner and dessert!

Mustard Toaster Pastries. Trust us. You have not lived until you've had a mustard-injected toasty treat while toking. Available in Cinnamon Sugar, Strawberry Frosted, and S'mores.

Nachos. We get it. Nothing beats nachos as the ultimate treat for the toasted. Our nachos come with salsa, pico de gallo, Wisconsin cheddar, jalapeños and sour cream. Just like with Cheesees, we've done our homework, and after extensive studies and employee-led taste tests, we've come up some classic combinations. Which one will be your favorite?

➢ Herring

➢ Skittles

➢ Pepperoni (substitute marinara for the salsa)

➢ Cookie dough

High Snackage

Go ahead and puff. We'll cook more stuff.

Chapter 9

The next day dawned clear, bright, and full of the promise of snow-melting warmth.

"Typical Utah," Brook told Neeta as they passed around coffee and slices of pumpkin pie she'd brought. "Just when you're ready to button down for a long cold spell, it gets beautiful again. By this afternoon, you won't even know its January."

"Not with pumpkin pie for breakfast!" Ted commented through a mouthful.

"This is Brook's idea of celebrating her first re-kill," the Z-Mat captain told them. "Any special occasion warrants pumpkin pie. Okay, if you can direct your attention to the screen…"

They were in one of the lodge conference rooms, a professional affair with a big oblong table and comfortable chairs. The Browns used their lodge for corporate retreats as well as skiing. Neeta winced when she saw one of the Z-Mat team drop a little whipped cream on the carpet. She hoped Altimeter Brown didn't see it, but his gaze was focused on the wall screen showing a map of the lodge with four blips moving along the slopes. He'd called her room first thing in the morning to tell her they'd found fresh ski trails on the snow where no one should have been skiing, so he had called Z-Mat, brought the ski patrol back to the lodge, and closed the lifts "for safety checks." He'd warned, however, that he would not hold that ruse for long.

Captain Lars moved his laser pointer to take in the more advanced slopes. "The local authorities are looking for Ethan. We've got all five remaining skiers on the slopes. Two are on Danger Zone, the double-black diamond slope; it's amazing how quick one's climbing back up after a run, even considering that zombies don't tire. We're guessing those are the Spars.

"Another is on Slippery Lip right now, probably Flannelette. According to SkiXtreme, she liked to warm up on the blues. The other is one of our snowboarders, and he's on the half-pipe park run. We're not sure about the fifth—the skier who was shot. He was with Flannelette, but disappeared into some trees and hasn't been seen for half an hour.

"Incidentally, Mr. Zwelleger was our shotgunner. He has been taken into custody until all this is over, so hopefully, we won't have any more trouble."

"Any of you good enough to behead a skiing zombie while shredding a double diamond?" Ted asked. When people responded with everything from shaking heads to eye rolls, he sighed. "Yeah, me neither."

Neeta could see him mentally adding it to his bucket list. Before he could suggest something that might make his wish a reality, she said, "We don't need to catch them on the run. We need to get them on the climb back up… or better yet…"

She turned to Altimeter. "How hard is it to work a lift?"

"See what I mean, babe? Who else gets to operate a ski lift on their vacation?"

Neeta warmed at the glee in Ted's voice as it came over her helmet headset. He was stationed at the first lift junction. From his point, it split into two lifts, one going to the black diamonds, the other to some higher blues and blacks. They'd decided to try to lure the zombies in with active lifts; what skier would want to waste time climbing the mountain when the lift would get them there easy and fast?

He had Brook and the captain with them, on the hopes of catching the Spars and perhaps Flannelette. Neeta remained on the ground slope, just in case any decided to take a run all the way down. She had crammed her hazmat suit under her snowsuit to look like a boarder instead of an exterminator, and the wrinkled fabric dug into her skin everywhere.

"Well, be careful up there," she said, shrugging her shoulders in a vain effort to set the fabric in place. She looked upslope, following the line of the lift moving slowly with empty seats. She wondered if Altimeter had told folks they were testing the equipment. She saw Ted wave. He had dressed as she had, although he could not get his hazmat gloves on under or over the ski gloves. Instead, he'd given the zombie-certified gloves to her to wear over her ski gloves.

"Sure thing. Hey, how's your plebe?"

She glanced at the Z-Mat rookie who held the lift throttle in a death grip while he scanned the area with quick, furtive glances. "Green. I'll talk to you later. Love you."

Once she'd hung up, she wandered back to Rookie, who had focused toward the lodge. "How's it going?"

He jumped. "Fine! Fine. I just... Does that snowman look right to you?" He pointed downslope to where the snowman stood several yards away, midway between them and the lodge.

"He looked better yesterday, that's for certain." The snowstorm of the day before had covered all the decorations in a thick layer of snow, which some kids had apparently tried to dust off this morning. The knit cap drooped, the T-shirt hung wrinkled and askew, and the Powerbar nose had slid until it more resembled a blockish goatee.

"No, I mean, there's something wrong with it—the snow. I just...I dunno...creepy."

Neeta peered closer Now that he'd mentioned it, there did seem to be a darker form under the snow and ice. Could it be Ethan?

She pulled out her sword, set the strap over her wrist, and started toward the snowman. It certainly wouldn't hurt anything to look—or to take its head off, for that matter. "Rookie, stay with the lift. Ted? It's me. We may have a dead one. Hang on, while I—"

The rookie shouted.

She spun, nearly losing her balance, and saw their shotgunned zombie skiing to the lift. Rookie backed away, training forgotten. He hadn't even pulled out his gun or his antifreeze. Neeta ran. "Stop the lift!"

"I, wha?" Rookie paused, confused. "Right! On it."

The zombie whacked the lever with his hand as he sped by. Its glove, which had been hanging free at the wrist, came off along with a couple of fingers. Fingers and glove fell into the mechanism. Neeta overtook Rookie but hurried past the lever and to the seats. If she could get to the zombie in time, she could chop him from the back before the lift carried him up, smooth and easy. Rookie could take the lever.

He boarded a seat. She ran behind the zombie, her sword activated. She swung.

"Look out!"

The oncoming seat caught her behind the knees, knocking her into the chair. Reflexively, she clutched at the bench with one hand. Her other hand, the one holding the activated sword, swung wide. It missed the zombie, but not its bench. The electrified monofilament sliced through the metal bars like butter before she could switch it off. The long bench tilted and spun toward her, flinging the zombie toward the ground. It reached out and grabbed her by the boot.

Neeta screamed as she slid from her chair. Only her gloved grip kept her from falling. She clawed frantically with her other hand for purchase, releasing her sword. It stopped short at the end of its strap, swinging and bumping the seat. Fortunately, it automatically turned off when she'd lost her grip. The lift continued forward, rising. The zombie pulled itself up, teeth snapping. She kicked at it with her free foot.

"Neeta!" Ted cried over her helmet.

"I can't stop it," Rookie said. "He jammed the controls!"

Their voices were faint compared to the snarls and growls of the corpsicle clutching her leg.

"Little busy!" Her muscles screamed from holding double-and-more of her body weight. She thought she felt pressure on her foot, chanced a quick look to see the zombie gnawing her snowboard boot while it clawed at her leg. He couldn't quite keep his grip on her with his damaged hand. She swung her free leg back, making the entire seat sway, and tried to smash the zombie in the face, but she couldn't connect.

Swearing in Korean, she took several quick, urgent breaths, steeled herself, and let go with her sword hand. With a flip of her wrist, she grabbed the handle and triggered it on. The monofilament unfolded, and the electric field charged with a reassuring hum. Her other arm protesting, fingers aching, she forced her legs up. Hours of hanging sit-ups paid off, and she lifted her feet and the zombie enough to arc her sword downward.

She only managed to remove part of its arm, but it was enough. The corpsicle gave a strangled yelp of surprise and fell.

Gasping with relief, she switched off the sword and grabbed the seat. It took three tries to pull herself up, and she clung to the armrest of the lift chair as she fought to get her breath back. At that moment the lift jerked to a stop, causing the chair to rock. She hugged the armrest tighter and pulled up the knee of her untouched leg, trying to angle as much of her weight to the back as possible, although she kept the leg that still bore the zombie's arm straight from her body to avoid contamination.

"I'm okay," she told herself, and then repeated it so the headset would pick it up. "Ted, I'm okay."

"Okay?" Ted yelped over the headset. "Woman, you are hot!"

After she had collected herself, Neeta peered over the back of the lift chair. The drop seemed to go forever. She pushed the thought out of her mind and focused on the zombie below, apparently still dazed from its fall. Good. Maybe it was too broken to move. Calmer now and grateful that the lift was still not moving, she braced her foot on the armrest to take some of her weight. "Ted, if the kids want to go bungee jumping, you'll have to take them!"

Ted laughed. "Anything you say, Boss. You were amazing! Just catch your breath while we deal with this corpsicle."

She knew his jubilant tone was for her benefit, but she couldn't stop herself from warning him to be careful. "I took off an arm, but the rest of it is intact."

"Gotcha. Brook will meet you at the top with a portable decontamination station for your boot."

She examined the leg the zombie had been clinging to. The boot was covered in tooth marks, but it hadn't broken the fabric or rubber. The part of the arm she'd cut off still clung to her pant leg. What a grip! At least it hadn't torn the suit, though they'd probably have to cut off part of it to get the arm off. Maybe she'd charge Brown for a new set of ski pants.

"When's my ride going to start?" Her arms were starting to protest.

Rookie answered. "Sorry. Any minute. Gotta be careful. We have to clear out the fingers."

With nothing better to do, she looked over the side to keep an eye on their fallen zombie. It struggled to stand and right its skis, which had miraculously survived the drop. By the time the lift started moving, the zombie had, too. As she headed uphill, her vantage point let her see another zombie speeding downslope. "Ted!"

"Easy, Boss. I got it."

She tore her eyes off the new zombie just as Ted did a showy twist of his sword and sliced her zombie through the neck. Captain Lars was watching him instead of keeping an eye on the surrounding area. They didn't know.

"Ted, behind you!"

The zombie whizzed by them, intent on speed rather than feed.

"Whoa! We see it!" She heard Ted and Lars making plans on the fly, and kept her mouth shut against the urge to micromanage.

The lift moved with painful slowness. Neeta strained to look behind and down to watch the progress of her fiancé, wincing as he caught up to the zombie and waved his arms at him as if to say, "That all you got?" and nearly lost his balance.

Why did he have to be such a goof? Why did she find it such a turn-on?

Be careful, she thought at him as he hurried down the slope. The captain, meanwhile, followed Ted's lead in teasing the zombie before heading toward the jump. Naturally, Ted's plan worked, and it followed. He had that talent—love him or hate him, he knew how to make people react, even dead ones.

Still, she had a bad feeling as he set himself up at the end of the picnic table and hollered encouragement to the two snowboarders. The lift finally came to an end and she jumped off.

Brook pushed the emergency stop button and set the bucket of disinfectant goop in front of her. When Neeta stuck her foot in it, she hit the timer on her watch. "Sixty seconds!" she said and knelt down by her to wrap a Hazmat bag around the zombie forearm. She tried to pull the fingers open, but they would not budge.

Neeta looked back. The captain had stopped on the ramp—but the zombie barreled into him, sending both flying in a tangle of arms and legs. "Hurry! Cut it off! I'll bill Brown for new pants. Brook, I need your board."

Brook fumbled with the scissors, finally having to use both gloved hands to work them as Neeta held the arm out of the way. She'd gotten her decontaminated boot in the bindings when she heard Ted's bloodcurdling scream.

Chapter 10

Ted's heart pounded as he watched his fiancé let go of the ski lift with one hand, raise her knees despite somewhere near two hundred pounds of corpse clinging to her legs, and swing Buffy. How could he feel so terrified and so turned on at the same time?

With a wordless shriek, the zombie plummeted to the slopes before him, and his woman scrambled to the seat, embracing it like he wanted to embrace her.

"I'm okay," she called, her voice breathy but strong, "but you have to take the kids bungee jumping."

One minute she's taking on a zombie midair, the next she's talking kids—oh, how he loved that woman! It was like marrying a superhero—minus the tawdry costumes. In public, anyway.

As he decapitated her disarmed zombie, he made a mental note to use that line sometime with her.

"Ted! Behind you!" she called. A zombie whizzed past with enough speed that Ted imagined it ruffled his ski suit. Behind him, Lars gave a shout of surprise. Why hadn't he seen it coming? Rookie!

Then again, I wasn't exactly thinking about my surroundings either. Neeta was so much better at that. Focus, Ted. Got to stay alive for the honeymoon.

"We see it!" he reported and pushed the image of Neeta in a skintight outfit of transparent Kevlar with a sky blue ZE on the chest. "So, Cap', if I get ahead, do you think you can herd it my way?"

"Head for the bottom of the jump," the captain said. They lowered their faceplates. As they started downhill, he explained. "That's Crown Spillanger. I used to follow his career. He loved jumps and never backs down from a challenge. I'll egg him on.

He'll take the ramp to the picnic table. That'll slow him."

"Awesome! How hard is it to land on a picnic table?" As they neared the corpse of Spillanger, Ted whooped and waved to get its attention.

"You nuts? I'll choke on the ramp, back off, and let it get all the glory—then you take it out. I'll follow."

"Just make sure you choke, then. I'll have my sword out and ready. I'll probably take it out at the legs first. Don't want to knee-capitate you instead."

Before Lars could reply, Ted put on some speed to get to the table first.

"Be ready—this thing's fast!" Lars called as Ted twisted to a backside stop beside the table and pulled out his sword. He freed one foot from the board to steady himself. His heart pounded with the adrenalin rush. He wished Neeta were on the other side of the bench to share this moment with him. "Bring it boys! Wooo!"

"On the ramp now. I—What the—!" Lars yelled.

Ted heard a crash and looked up.

Zombie and captain were flying toward him.

He switched off the sword just as they crashed into him. One of the boards splintered itself on his helmet, dazing him for a moment as they all fell to the ground. They tumbled down the hill, he and Lars flailing in an effort to knock the zombie off them but only succeeding in smacking each other. He thought he heard Neeta shout. Pain lanced through his pinkie finger.

They slid partway down the hill before a mogul halted their progress. The captain rolled away, choking and cussing. The zombie lay broken beside Ted, but when it saw him, it crawled forward, groaning, "Shaaaame!"

Ted activated the sword and took off the top half of its head. It gave a last strangled gasp and fell still.

Ted flopped his head back on the snow and took inventory. Legs twisted, but okay. His head rung. Bruised rib, maybe broken—and wow, his hand…

He raised his arm and saw the pinkie of his ski glove covered in blood.

"Shit!" He sat up, ignoring the vertigo, and wiped the glove off in the clean snow away from the zombie. He winced. It felt broken. It looked like the tip had been torn off.

Or bitten.

He didn't bother to think. Thinking would mean hesitation, and if he hesitated, he'd lose his nerve, and maybe his life—and he had way too much to live for. He set his hand on the cold snow, pinkie extended and the others curled, and activated his sword

The electrified blade slashed through his finger. He screamed.

When Neeta got to the scene, the captain was dragging Ted away from the zombie spoor. She couldn't see Ted's face, but his strangled gasps and the way he kept a death grip on his hand made her heart catch in her throat. "Ted?"

"I got the corpsicle," he managed to choke out. "No worries!"

The captain looked up. "Fill your helmet with snow, now!"

She kicked free of her board, ignoring it as it slid downhill, and yanked off her helmet, filling it with the freshest snow she could find. She ran to where he had set Ted against a tree and was pulling off Ted's helmet. Ted snatched her helmet and shoved his hand into the snow before she could see the damage. She crouched beside him and stroked back his sweaty hair. She'd never seen his face so pale. It almost matched the snow. "What happened?"

Ted's smile was mostly grimace. "I gave the zombie the finger."

"What?" She spun to the remains of the creature and saw among some melted and re-freezing snow a bloody, glove-covered finger. "Ted!" She rose to retrieve it, but he lashed out and grabbed her arm.

"Leave it." He gasped. "Might have been bit. Could have been a board. My sword. Figured, better safe. Oh, if I die, don't put that on my tombstone!"

"You're not going to die!" Nonetheless, she started running through the signs of zombieism as she set her hand on his forehead. She hoped he'd think she was being reassuring rather than checking for fever.

He forced a strained laugh. "Everybody dies, babe. How about 'Safe was sorry'?"

"How about dying after you tell this story to our grandkids?" Cool forehead. Probably shock setting in. He must have used his sword to cut off his own finger. It would have cauterized the wound. At least he wouldn't bleed to death. She blinked back tears as she pulled off her jacket to wrap him up. She didn't care if that got contaminated. She'd add it to Brown's account.

"Then I need a fuzing nickname. Grandpa Nine Fingers?" His eyelids drooped.

She had to keep him talking. "How about 'Pinky'?"

"Pinky? You're killing me, babe."

"Frodo?"

He managed a snort.

They traded nicknames and lame one-liners for his tombstone until the ski patrol strapped him into a sled and sped him to a waiting ambulance.

Two nurses and the emergency room doctor met the ambulance. They hustled Ted through the emergency room doors, the doctor calling out for a second IV bag and checking the dressings while the nurses made sure he was securely strapped down.

"We have a room ready," the doctor said. "Mr. Hacker, can you hear me? Are you in pain? Would you like more morphine?"

Ted gave the doctor a dopey smile. "Morphine good! Hey, will I be able to play the piano?"

Neeta hustled along with the rest, her hand on Ted's leg so he'd know she was with him. Could he even feel her grip under all the blankets? They'd doffed their outfits and hurried through the decontamination. She was double glad for the Z-mat's foresight in getting the fast-acting stuff. Her hair was still damp and she was freezing again, but none of that mattered. Ted had to be okay, and she wouldn't leave him until she knew that he was. No one objected as she followed them to the tiny, bare room.

Sheriff Rourke waited at the door with Deputy Benjy.

Rourke joined her. "Neeta."

She gave Ted a reassuring smile before following Rourke to a corner of the room.

He jerked his head toward Ted, who was telling the nurse taking his blood that he didn't know how to play the piano. "I'm so sorry about this," Rourke said.

Neeta swallowed hard and tensed against the desire to tremble, even if Rourke might attribute it to the cold.

"Risks of the job. We still don't know if he was bitten or just injured. He didn't wait to find out—and even if he has been bit, his fast action might have saved him. Kind of like cutting off a finger to prevent a snake bite poison—except zombie contagion moves more slowly."

She begged her words to be true. There had only been one reported survivor of the zombie virus, and he'd injected himself. No one knew for certain if he had some kind of immunity or if the virus had died in storage. At any rate, it was a special case. No one who had been bitten ever escaped contagion.

Rourke seemed to read her thoughts. "If it doesn't work, though… Can you?"

An eerie calm settled over her. She and Ted had talked about this when she'd first hired him and then again after their engagement. They had a pact. She met his eyes. "Yes. I'm an exterminator. Part of the job."

He nodded, one professional to another. "'Kay, then. Benjy will be outside, though. Just in case."

"Sensible." She couldn't make herself say more.

Again, he gave her a nod and left.

The nurse had set Ted up with a second IV drip to start when the first one finished and hooked him up to an EKG. Other than that, the room held nothing but a chair. Ted snored in morphine-induced slumber, a raucous accompaniment to the steady beep of the EKG.

The nurse took a blood sample from Neeta, too, just in case, while the doctor pointed to the EKG and told her, "That way, you'll have some warning if he expires when your attention's elsewhere. You look chilled. I'll have an orderly bring you something warm from the cafeteria."

The doctor hurried to follow the nurses out. Neeta grabbed his arm and spun him back to face her.

"Wait a minute! That's it? What about his hand?"

"His hand? He may have been bitten by a zombie, and you're worried about his hand?" The doctor looked at her as if she were daft. He'd already written her man off as a shambler in waiting!

He pulled toward the door as he spoke. She tightened her grip on his arm to hold him still. He might outweigh her by a hundred pounds, but years on her job made had given her muscles of steel while his more resembled jelly.

"Or he may not have been bit. We don't know. You're not even going to clean the wound? What about cell stimulation? You're just going to leave him like that? He's not even in a real hospital bed!"

The doctor gritted his teeth, then spoke in clipped tones. "Look, he's a potential bite victim. You, of all people, should know how this works. Under the zombie rider of the Better Health Care for All Americans Act, in case of suspected bites, hospitals must first ensure the safety of staff by isolating the victim and keeping him under guard. As for care, we're required to provide only basic comfort until a blood screening removes any doubt of infection. He's comfortable, he has access to plenty of morphine, and he won't die from the injury, so unless you have additional insurance other than what the Government Standard that his card indicates?"

Neeta released his arm before she squeezed bruises into it. "When will the blood test come back?"

"Tomorrow morning."

"Tomorrow?"

"The mail has gone out, and we don't have the authorized funds for something like this. If he's infected, a few more hours won't mean anything."

"And if he's not, what will that mean for his hand?"

Just as he started to edge toward the door while blustering again about priorities and regulations tying his hands, a gentle knock sounded on the door. Mandy Brown poked her head in.

Neeta gaped. "What do you want?"

Mandy smiled at the doctor. "May I come in, Carlton? It's just, I thought Neeta might want some family to comfort her in this time…"

Carlton brightened at the change of subject. "I didn't realize."

"Half-sisters, actually, and it was kind of a surprise," Mandy kept her simpering smile trained on the doctor, ignoring Neeta's glower. "How are Vicki and the kids?"

Carlton turned his back on Neeta and stepped toward Mandy, his need to leave suddenly forgotten. "Fine, fine. And Tim?"

She lowered her head, tsking. "So stressed about the resort and the contest. I mean, what horrid luck that zombies should arise now."

"You should have dug those skiers up last year," Neeta cut in. "Why don't you continue your chat outside?" She gripped her sword, wishing it were her chainsaw. It was so much more satisfying to threaten people with a chainsaw.

Mandy spoke over her. "You know what would really cheer Tim up? A chance to fly his helicopter. He adores that thing. He brought me down from Ute2, but you know how short a trip that is. Now, I couldn't help but overhear, and I know it's a bit irregular, but what if he were to fly those blood samples to the CDC in Salt Lake? Free of charge, of course. Neeta is family, and it would settle Tim's nerves so."

What? Neeta slumped while the doctor shifted his weight from one foot to another and made squeaky sounds. Over his shoulder, Mandy gave Neeta a quick wink.

"He'll have to take an orderly," he said at last.

"Of course. I'll stay with Neeta, if that's all right."

The doctor gave her an alarmed look. "But the zombie!"

"Potential!" Neeta snarled.

Mandy held up placating hands. "Neeta is the consummate professional. I'm completely confident in her. So you'll make the arrangements? Oh, God bless you, Carlton, God bless you!" She slipped her arm though his and led him the couple of steps to the door. She even gave him a little princess wave before shutting the door and leaning against it. She raised her eyes to the ceiling, though Neeta couldn't tell if she was expressing exasperation or seeking strength from a Higher Power.

"Phew! You'll have to forgive Carlton. He's one of my flock. He lost his private practice for providing 'unwarranted and unauthorized care' to an elderly patient; the hospital hired him for the emergency room, but they've made it clear he's not to cross the line. He's really a very good surgeon. It won't take half an hour to get that blood work to Salt Lake. We'll find out in a couple of hours. Oh, Neeta!"

The shakes Neeta had been fighting since seeing Ted lying in the snow—since the zombie attacked her on the lift—finally asserted themselves. Mandy threw her arms around Neeta, supporting her as she led her to the chair by Ted's gurney. She settled her there and placed one of Neeta's hands on Ted's shoulder. "Now, you just sit. I'm going to get us some hot coffee—do you like it with cream? Black? All right. I'll get us some coffee, and we'll wait together. You don't even need to talk to me."

"I…" Neeta swallowed the lump in her throat. "Thank you."

"Not at all. It's the least I could do after making such a botch of our meeting. I always imagined what it would be like to meet as sisters, but never did I imagine you didn't know… Oh, that's not important now! Coffee. I'll be right back."

Neeta watched her go, feeling cold and numb. What had just happened? Snarky Mandy Culvert being nice? Maybe she was a parson, after all.

Ted stirred, and she rose and stepped back, just in case. His eyes fluttered open—normal, clear, the eyes she loved to gaze into. She felt a hot tear escape and rubbed her cheek fast before he noticed. "The piano joke, really?"

"Blame the morphine," he whispered. He pulled weakly at the restraints holding his wrists.

She set her hand over his good one. "Just until the blood tests get back."

He nodded, and then seemed to go away for a minute. She caressed his hand and waited. He was getting his color back. Although not definite, it was a good sign.

"Is this a bad time to say you look good enough to eat?" he asked.

Tears blurred her vision. She blinked them away. "That's not funny!"

"Was in San Francisco."

"That's when we thought I was infected." She sniffled. Now, she had a glimmer of how he must have felt as they'd waited for her blood work to come back that day. Of course, she'd been conscious, and he'd put all his energy into distracting her with lame jokes.

Just like now. "Ah, double standard then. You know, if this were a movie, we'd have to have a romantic, bittersweet wedding right here and now."

Despite herself, she laughed. "How about the song? Parson Brown will be back with coffee in a couple of minutes. She can do the job."

"Honeymoon could be a problem." He pulled at the straps, directing her attention to them. "Unless you're into this sort of thing."

She sniffled again and scrubbed her eyes. "I don't know about the honeymoon, but there's a certain appeal to you not being able to get into trouble."

His eyelids began to droop. She kissed his head. "Get some sleep. It'll be okay."

"You don't know that." His voice was as serious as she'd ever heard.

She answered with all her steel. "I refuse to believe otherwise."

"Neeta, if it isn't… If I… Can you?"

She pulled out her sword so he could see it. He smiled.

"Good. I want it to be someone I trust."

He sighed and gave himself to sleep while Neeta indulged herself with a few tears before her half-sister   returned.

Chapter 11

Brook Bridges hammered in a pole on her side of the slope's picnic table, then fastened razor wire to it and handed the spool to the captain. Around them, members of the ski patrol were booby-trapping ski jumps and other obstacles.

"I think you and Ted had the right idea, but the execution proved too tricky," she told the captain. "This way, we let the wire take out the zombies at the shins, while we stand back and hack them after they've toppled."

Lars shook his head, impressed. With three zombies left on the slopes and a possible fourth—the boyfriend—at large, and their experienced exterminators out of the picture for a while, he hadn't been sure how his Z-Mat team would be able to take them all out. Yet after seeing Ted off in the ambulance, he'd come back to find Brook hard at work directing the ski patrol in trap-setting while the Z-Mat team searched the slopes. If the traps worked, Brook would have significantly cut their danger level.

"You're getting a commendation for this."

"Really? Thanks! I know it's kind of sick, but this has been a dream day, you know? All that training, and I didn't think I'd ever get to go up against the undead."

He grunted and concentrated on tying the wire to hide his guilt. Twice she'd volunteered for exterminator duty in Afghanistan, and twice he'd refused to send her. He hadn't thought Brook could cut it. Guess I misjudged her. Not such a scam after all. We need to change her nickname. Hack? Edge? Slice!

A shout of warning from above made them both hustle away from the table as a zombie approached at high speed—Flannelette. It jumped, pulling its knees up to lift the board, and hit the table at a half spin that led it to a horizontal slide just as its legs came to the razor wire.

Instead of knocking it flat however, the super-sharp wire sliced through suit, flesh and all. The zombie pinwheeled its arms, as its legless body flipped. It landed downslope of the table with a thunk and a small cloud of snow. Afterward, it lay there, moaning, "Faaaail!"

Lars examined the label on the spool he held: Wire by Ginsu. Caution: edges lined with monofil-ament. Handle with specialized gloves. Able to cut a tin can and still slice your tomatoes! NOT A TOY. He cringed and checked his hands to be sure he had all his fingers.

Meanwhile, Brook hurried forward, pulling her ax from its sheath. Lars shook his head, bemused, as she used both hands to slice through its neck. Chop. Yeah. "Chop" was the right name.

"Look!" Brook pointed down the hill to where the legs were still moving, guiding the snowboard until it tried to take on another obstacle and, lack-ing knees, it plopped over, twitching as the feet tried to right the board.

"That's what I call muscle memory!"

"I can't believe your mother said you were a mistake."

Neeta sighed. Despite Mandy's promise to sit quietly with her, she only seemed able to hold her silence for a few minutes before bringing up their past—and always with the worst possible spin. The "couple of hours" had stretched into three, and she had twice heard Benjy sending away some nosy reporter looking for an interview; or maybe a photographer hoping to snap a pic of her decapitating her fiancé. She wouldn't put it past them. She knew she would have to explain why she hadn't done that in the first place. Someone would bring up Bergie; they always did.

She just wanted time to think, to steel herself for the worst. But no, Parson Mandy Brown wanted to "support her dear half-sister," and for some reason, Neeta could not turn her away.

"She didn't say that," Neeta answered with asperity. "She said being with my—our—father was a mistake. I was the fortunate consequence of a rash action. Look, Mandy, you've got this tragic, depressing life story all thought up for me, but you're wrong, okay? I never pined for a father. My mom was happy with just us and her career, and I was, too. I had Uncle Jerry and Aunt XiaXia and their kids were my brothers and sisters. I didn't want your family. I never even thought about your family."

"But you seemed so sad and, well, angry when we showed up."

Sudden anger, old and new, flashed through Neeta, and only Ted snoring in his gurney kept her from jumping up and shouting. "Yes! Because you showed up right after we buried Uncle Jerry. I wanted to be with my best friend Min, and instead I was ordered to entertain you while our mothers fought—and all you wanted to do was go on about your daddy loving you best."

"You never said!"

"It was none of your business. Besides, it was splattered all over the news. I'd already had to deal with strangers I didn't want, and then you took me away from my friends."

Ted tried to roll over in his sleep, making the leather and Velcro of the straps creak. Neeta got up and turned her back on Mandy to stroke his hair and check again for signs of fever.

Mandy asked in a small voice. "Am I taking you from Ted now?"

Neeta closed her eyes, the better to concentrate on the silkiness of Ted's hair before answering. "No. Maybe, but in this case, I'd probably just be worrying, anyway. It's fine. But as soon as Ted wakes up…"

"I'm out of here. No problem. What if he…?"

Neeta caressed her sleeping fiancé's hair. "Then you run, and tell Deputy Benjy to get ready with a double tap in case I fail."

After another hour, even Mandy's nonstop conversation had dribbled into silence. She sat still in the cheap chair, hands folded—praying, Neeta guessed. What would it be like to pray that easily?

She wished she could have that kind of peace. Still, who knew how Mandy would be acting if their roles were reversed and she sat beside her husband on what could be a death watch-and-rekill op?

Neeta resisted the urge to remove the wrappings on Ted's bandaged hand to search for decay. The EMTs had wrapped it, but no one had touched it since. Had they taken his glove off? She couldn't remember, but apparently, it wasn't enough to worry about until they knew if he was infected or not. She gritted her teeth. Where were those lab results?

She wet a napkin with some water from the carafe Mandy had gotten along with the second chair and wiped his brow. A thin sheen of sweat covered his face, and he grimaced in his sleep. Pain, or the first effects of the contagion? What if he'd only gotten a little infected, and his body was fighting it? No one had ever survived a bite, even after cutting off the infected area, but Ted was stubborn and crazy enough to be the first.

I should call the Zombie Institute. If he's infected, they'd want to study the transformation—and they'd probably treat his hand, regardless.

No. They'd probably medevac him to one of their labs in Vegas, and she'd have to go back to the slopes. If he reanimated, and she wasn't there…

He'd asked her to do it, to end it for him. It might be his last request.

What was taking so long?

To hell with it; I'm taking off the bandages and checking myself. Besides, then they'll have to put on fresh dressings, if nothing else. She laid the napkin flat on his head. "Hey, Mandy."

Mandy jumped. "Is he?"

"No, no! I just need you to get a nurse."

A knock on the door interrupted her, and both ladies froze, watching it open with hope and expectation.

A sad-eyed man in a cheap business suit and a bulky tablet years out of date stepped in and closed the door behind him. He looked at Neeta and smiled the most piteous smile she'd seen since... A vision of a funeral flashed over her mind and she felt her stomach clench.

Basset Eyes held out his hand. "Neeta Lyffe! I'm a big fan, a big fan."

She blinked, her train of thought derailed—a relief, but confusing, nonetheless. "Excuse me? Did you sneak in here for an autograph?"

"No. I'm sorry. I'm just a bit of a fan boy of ZDE, I suppose." He made it sound like a death knell. "I'm Roderick Nips, your court-appointed grief counselor."

"My what?" Behind Nips' shoulder, Mandy gave a little wave and pointed at the door. As she turned to leave, Neeta felt the sudden urge to call her back. She closed her eyes, collected her wits, and walked around the bed to shake his proffered hand. "My grief counselor? But…"

"Oh, I know you didn't qualify when your mother died, but it turns out with the lawsuit draining your funds, this time you do you qualify financially for government assistance during this time of emotional need. Isn't that lucky?" He gave her a tragic, sympathetic grin that would have made babies cry, then turned his attention to his tablet. "Now, there are several programs that -"

"But Ted -" Neeta interrupted.

He held up a hand. "I realize you aren't married, but with the 'What's Marriage Compared to Love' Act almost passed, I'm sure we can work something out. As I was saying, there are some forms."

"He's not dead yet!"

He stopped, blinking as she had only moments before, then squinted first at Ted, then at her. "Oh, well, I'd just assumed that after what you did to Bergie…"

Six hours ago, she'd been hanging from a ski lift, holding on for dear life while trying to kick a zombie off her leg. That was now looking like the highlight of her day. Ted's pained face, Mandy's poetic fantasy for her life, the waiting, the hospital... Something snapped, and before she knew it, she had Nips pinned against the wall, her forearm against his throat. His pad slipped from his hands and hit the floor with a single heavy thunk.

"Now you listen to me, Mr. Big Fan, because I'm only saying this once, understand?" she growled. It felt good.

He nodded, his droopy eyes now the size of saucers.

"Maybe you didn't notice, or maybe you were too busy enjoying the show to care, but Donald Eidelberg was biter buffet before we could do anything about it. There was no doubt of his infection. Ted took every precaution—even slicing off his own gorram finger!—to avoid contagion. Got that?"

Nips made a strangled gurgle. She took that as yes.

"Look around you? Do you see a swarm about to overtake us if we wait?"

"Nggh."

"Do you see a bunch of half-trained plebes ready to bolt and make themselves next on the menu?"

He wheezed.

"What I did on that show saved the lives of seven plebes and two cameramen. Maybe you thought I got a kick out of beheading a friend?"

"He begged for mercy," Nips croaked.

"I gave it to him."

She jerked away, and he buckled over, gasping more from fright than the need for air. She knew her strength and hadn't been holding him that hard, not that she'd ever tell him that. "I don't need your services. You want to help, Big Fan, then you tell a nurse to get in here with new dressings and an extra pair of gloves. Now, go!"

He gathered up his pad and ran. She glared at the door, daring Deputy Benjy to come in and ask what happened.

From behind her, a voice croaked, "Did that feel as good to do as it did to watch?"

"Ted!" She spun and hurried to his side. She poured some water in the bottle and held the straw to his lips so he could sip. Her hands trembled as she set the bottle down on the table by his head, but she treated him to a smile she hoped didn't look as tragic as Nips' had. "How are you feeling?"

"Hand's burning. I could use some morphine—though your little show was quite distracting. I was waking up as he came in. You're so hot when you get feisty. You know, I had thought about groaning, 'Braaaains,' to see if I could get him to wet his pants, but I think you did that." Pain dulled his expression and belied the humor in his voice.

She giggled. Tears burned her eyes and nose but didn't spill over. "Good thing you didn't; I'd have probably spun around and beheaded you on the spot."

"All grace and lethal ballet." His attempt at a lusty grin ended in a grimace.

"I'll get Benjy to fetch the nurse."

She opened the door. Nips was talking to Deputy Benjy, his arms waving in animated yet somehow, depressed motions. Further down the hallway, however, the doctor hurried toward her with a nurse and an orderly pushing a cart. Mandy trotted beside them and when she saw Neeta, she waved.

"The tests were negative, Neeta! He's all right!"

Neeta sagged against the threshold. Thank you, Lord. Thank you.

LinnAnn Pike settled more comfortably in her wheelchair and re-adjusted the blanket covering her knees. She hadn't wanted to come outside, but as soon as she'd seen that cop enter the lodge, asking for her, she'd told Kevin to handle it and hightailed it to the porch. Guns made her nervous, especially when worn by cismale authority figures. They'd legalized marijuana. How hard could it be to outlaw guns?

Well, Kevin will take care of it for me, and I won't have to know a thing about it. He knows my old heart can't take any kind of shock. Besides, idiot will forget three minutes after the conversation ends.

She thought longingly of her youth, when she wore a bikini and brought in customers to the medical marijuana tents of Venice Beach. Those had been the days—hanging out on the boardwalk, suggesting to passersby that she had the cure for their stress, long evenings on the beach, learning the mysteries of weed and how it could be claimed on government insurance forms. Those forms always made so much more sense after some heavy toking. But no, she had to fall in love with a hardcore skier, and now she spent her winters hanging out at the lodge where he ran his ski shop. Her bikini days were long gone; the locals called her "Grandma" now.

Speaking of, where was that no-good grandson of hers, anyway? Usually, he made a stop on Fridays to get a supply of good stuff, but she hadn't seen him since she told him he needed to start paying. Probably off with that tramp of a girlfriend… Ah well, young love—and it is turning out to be a nice day for it.

The wind still held a bite to it, but the sun has come out and the air had warmed—enough, even, to melt the snowman, she noticed. She regarded the sculpture thoughtfully, snickering because the power bar had run down its face, leaving a chocolate stripe and settling somewhere suggestive and obscene. Water dripped off its outstretched hands. Whoever had built it had done a fantastic job, but she had to wonder why she or he hadn't come to take credit.

Maybe the zombie scare drove her or him off. After the ambulance carted that guy away, the resort officials couldn't hide it any longer. Some people had left; others were scrambling to find good viewing spots in hopes of catching a shambler on their camera phones—apparently, the

ZomBlog was offering free T-shirts and other prizes for video of the skiing and snowboarding zombies. Still others, however, hung around, hoping that the Z-Mat team and those California exterminators could clear the slopes in time for the contest tomorrow. Naturally, plenty of those people were feeling the stress. Thanks to the national legalization of marijuana, she had the cure, no medical excuse necessary but insurance gladly charged, and everyone trusted Grandma for the best.

She leaned forward and took her blunt from the ashtray. It was a hassle to sit outside to smoke, but it was her best advertising, even if most people preferred the sanitized pill form. Philistines. So worried about lung damage. Didn't they know that was tobacco? She drew in a long pull from her joint, smiling at the people walking by on the porch before hacking up some phlegm. In her youth, that smile and a big deep breath would have brought guys running asking for a sample. Getting old stunk!

A few people glanced at her sandwich-board sign, but otherwise the only reaction she got was the not-so-polite cough-cough of a prissy nonsmoker. Her grin widened, and she opened her mouth as she inhaled through her nose, pulling the smoke out of her mouth and into her nostrils, just like she'd seen in the old movies her mother loved. She thought of it as recycling; it always turned her husband Hank on, but at the moment, she enjoyed a spark of glee to see the disgusted look on Prissy Nonsmoker's face. Reminded her of her daughter-in-law…well, ex daughter-in-law. Best part of that divorce was she never had to talk to her again, especially after the uptight control freak found out LinnAnn was covering for her grandson. In fact, she had a special ringtone just to warn her should that little witch ever get the urge to call.

She followed Miss Prissy with her gaze, keeping up the trick and enjoying her reaction, until the couple passed by the snowman. Surprise made her gasp. The smoke tried to enter and exit both her nostrils and throat at the same time, making her cough.

Did she just see its hand move?

Maybe too much recycling… She blinked to clear her vision and focused. Wait. Yes. Maybe. She called her assistant to watch the "shop" while she wheeled herself down the ramp to investigate. At the bottom of the ramp, tied to framework with a bike chain, waited her walker. She pointed her fob at it, and with a click and a beep, the chain fell away.

Stupid faulty sense of balance, she grumbled as she stood, folded her wheelchair and tied it with the chain. She set the walker into the ground with a firm push. Hank had had it specially made for her with tiny spikes to dig into the snow and ice so she wouldn't slip. The handles had pads against the cold. She still didn't like needing it. Still, it did accord her certain deferences, like now, as two handsome young boarders approached to see if she needed help.

"Would you escort me to the snowman, please?" She batted her eyes and gave her sweet grandma look. "I don't need help, really, but I'd so appreciate your company." After all, she may be a married septuagenarian, but she wasn't dead, yet.

It was only a few dozen yards to the snowman, but she took her time. The boys paced her patiently enough—one of the things she liked about Utah, real respect for their elders here—and when they arrived at the snowman, politely excused themselves to go check their boards.

"Wait!" she grabbed one's arm, not because she wanted his company, but because she was right— the hand had moved! Or rather, the fingers trapped inside the ice had wiggled. She studied the fingers, hand, arm, taking in hints of motion. She wanted to be sure before she asked the boys to verify what she saw. She didn't want to seem crazy after all— that's bad for business, her business, especially. Still, she thought she heard a low moaning: aaaaay…

She took a step closer, rubbed some of the snow off the snowman's face with her gloved hand and saw the mouth move. Even worse, she recognized the face!

"Quick! Get help! That's my grandson in there!"

Chapter 12

With everyone reassured that Ted would not die and come back, a nurse hustled Neeta out of the room while they worked on his hand.

"It's okay, babe," Ted said when she hesitated. "Go take care of the actual undead. I'll be here, alive and waiting, when you get back."

Alive. She liked that word! She gave him a quick kiss and left, her heart light.

Mandy and Benjy waited outside the door.

"Tim's got the chopper warmed up and ready to take us home," Mandy said and led them down the hall. Neeta hung back with Benjy to thank him for standing watch and to get an update on the zombie situation.

"Last call I got was about half an hour ago," the deputy said. "They'd managed to take out the two females using a modified version of Ted's original idea. They'd set wire traps. One got tangled and they took it out, but the other apparently sliced off its own legs. Wish I could have seen that!"

Neeta laughed along with him. These were good people, and for having no practical experience, they adapted quickly. "So two left?"

He nodded. "Ethan—the boyfriend who was probably bit by one of the team—and Tom Spars. He's avoided every obstacle so far. He's world class—or was when he was alive."

"Sounds like it still is. We're going to need a better trap. Did anyone know him alive, even by reputation? Also, what are the chances someone else has been infected? Have you checked missing persons?"

"No one we can associate with the zombies. We got lucky so far."

Neeta nodded. "How about the zombies themselves? Any indication any of them has eaten other than the one who got Ethan?"

Benjy's brows knit in thought, then he paled. "I don't think we looked!"

She set a reassuring arm on his shoulder. "It's okay; they've been on the slopes, mostly, but have someone check before they dispose of the bodies. There'd be fresh blood on their faces or outfits. Swab the mouth for multiple blood types; check the stomach contents. The one I'm most concerned about is Ethan. Who knows where he'll show up."

She felt a sudden foreboding. She was missing something, something about Ethan?

Benjy saw her frown. "Don't worry. We've alerted his hometown. People know to stay away from him."

"This is Chill Winters with Extreme Sports. Even though the Operation Homefront/Ute2 HotDoggers Competition has been put on hold due to Utah's most extreme zombie outbreak in history, we are here to catch the action—and right now, that action is at the lodge with an extreme rescue being led by LinnAnn Pike, known locally as Grandma."

Chill pointed her mike at the septuagenarian in an imported snowsuit with marijuana leaf patterns and "Grandma Grows Best" embroidered on the pocket.

LinnAnn grinned uncomfortably at the camera while trying to keep an eye on the crowd behind her. People took turns pointing hair dryers at her frozen grandson. A couple of folks started to dig and chip at the snow around him. They'd managed to get the hand thawed, and it grasped at the air, fingers and wrist working.

People had gathered around them, both spectators, other news crews, and a small group bearing signs protesting Global Cooling. Sunstealers!, WalkWarm Causes Global Cooling!, Global Cooling Kills! and others. One had "Warming" crossed out and "Cooling" written in its place, and a few had Global Fattening boards instead. When the noise of the crowd lulled, they could hear a low moan coming from the snowman.

"It's just happenstance that I saw him this morning," LinnAnn said. "I have no idea why he'd have been out in the storm—probably ran away from home. After his parents got divorced, I'm the one he turned to. I just hope we can save him now.

Hey!" She yelled at the boys with shovels. "Are you nuts? He's frozen in there. What if you take off a toe? He's probably got hypothermia or something—let's just do this slow and easy! Aim for the face! Let's help him breathe!"

She excused herself to oversee the zealous idiots thawing out her boy. She heard Chill use that as a segue to talk about how her grandson could possibly alive. Chill's interviewee, a handsome, swarthy man from WalkWarm Outerwear of Patagonia, apparently had the answer. In perfect English with just enough Latin accent to be sexy, he told Chill how fortunate Ethan was that his grandmother had bought him a WalkWarm ski suit.

The rescue group had stopped chopping and was concentrating on warming Ethan for the moment, so LinnAnn turned to listen. That guy was so gorgeous. Even a couple of the protestors—two girls and a gay guy if she was any judge—were edging closer to him.

If she was just 20 years younger...

"The suit is more than stylish," the Latin spokesman insisted. "The monofilaments absorb kinetic and solar energy, convert it to heat, and gradually transfer that energy to the interior of the suit for the body to absorb. We've done extensive tests, and WalkWarm is used even by science teams in Antarctica as well as by Chinese taikonauts, but never had we expected a situation like this."

Chill nodded. "Talk about extreme conditions!"

The spokesman laughed. "I can only guess the suit had gathered a great deal of energy. Even with the sunny days Utah has enjoyed, our friend here must have been skiing hard or running."

"So why don't we see these amazing suits in ski boutiques or on Bellerophon?"

Suddenly, the protestors pushed the spokesman aside.

"The technology is banned! Don't let him fool you!" The boy declared. LinnAnn sighed. Not gay, then. Just an idiot.

"The suit steals energy from the sun—just like solar panels did in the turn of the century!" one of the girls added. "Our misguided attempts at cheap, fast energy have caused Global Cooling. We should be banning it."

"Ban WalkWarm! It Causes Global Cooling!" the third one chanted, and the rest joined in.

Sexy Spokesman spread his arms and declared to no one that the US had already banned Walk-Warm sales.

"His mouth is clear!" someone behind her hollered, and she turned from the spectacle and back to her grandson. As the cameras focused in, the man scraped at the snow around the mouth.

The defrosting zombie snapped at him. The man yelped and jerked his hand away, ripping his glove. "Oh, my heck! The dude tried to bite me!"

Grandma LinnAnn pushed him aside and reached into her pocket to pull out a fat joint. "He's panicking. Here, honey. This will help you relax."

He snapped his teeth, just missing her hand.

"Quit clowning around, boy. This is Christmas blend—some of my best stuff." She lit it and waved it under his nose.

"AAAaaaaaaii…"

"Yes, Ace, dear. The very best. Relax and take it in; there's a good boy." Carefully, she set the joint into his mouth. Reflexes took hold and his lips curled around the blunt. He stilled, puffing and cooing to himself. Cloves and cinnamon added to the smell of cannabis and decay.

"Naaa…"

"That's right. Nonnny nonny nana…"

In LinnAnn's pocket, her phone sang out, playing, "I didn't mean to break your heart (Actually, I did)." She ignored it. It was her ex-daughter-in-law. The woman hadn't talked to her in years, and she chooses now to call? Anything that awful mother had to tell her could wait while she took care of her grandson.

Neeta and Mandy emerged onto the helipad to find a crowd of reporters and cameramen aching for quotes about the infestation and Ted's prognosis. Years of PR work for Zombie Death Extreme and HumVans took over, enabling Neeta to give a quick interview as they hustled to the waiting chopper. She even managed to plug Operation Homefront, asking folks to check their website and donate through there. That earned her a hug from Mandy and praise from the competition organizer, who was waiting for her in the helicopter. Altimeter, however, just glared.

"Don't expect gratitude from me until you've cleared out those zombies and I can get back to business," he snarled.

That worked fine for Neeta, but Mandy snarled back at him and told him to show some respect, and the organizer chimed in that Neeta had an interview with Extreme Sports first, and soon the noise of their arguing drowned out the sound of the chopper blades. In fact, Neeta would have loved a nice calming whuppa-whuppa-whuppa to Mandy's harpy shrieks, Altimeter's roaring, and the Peterson's overstressed rational tones. By the time the helicopter came in sight of the Ute2 lodge, Neeta was looking forward to a nice, relaxing day of chasing zombies on skis and removing their heads. Despite her trepidation concerning heights, she looked out the window and noticed a crowd not far from the lodge.

"What's going on around the snowman?" she asked. The feeling of foreboding returned.

"That's what I've been trying to say!" Peterson said. "Turns out it's a frozen man!"

"Frozen man? Can someone survive that?" Many asked.

Neeta's heart pounded. She'd been planning to check that snowman.

Peterson crowed. "They say he was wearing WalkWarm. That's one of our sponsors. See, Tim?

I told you bringing them in would work in our favor."

Mandy handed Neeta binoculars.

People were pointing—were those hair dryers?—at the frozen man while an old woman with a walker stroked his head. The outstretched hand had defrosted to the elbow and moved in short, jerky motions that set Neeta's hackles rising.

Peterson continued, "It's amazing publicity. Extreme Sports is filming; they're calling it the extreme rescue. He's puffing a joint while they thaw the rest of it out."

The druggie boyfriend. Ethan! Neeta's stomach gave a lurch that had nothing to do with acrophobia. "Tim! Tell those people to get away from him. That's not a man—that's a zombie!"

Melted snow flowed in rivulets down Ethan's face, tracing little rivers in the snow still holding his body imprisoned before spreading in a wide puddle at his feet. Grandma LinnAnn noticed one side looked a little pinkish.

"Is one of you idiots chipping away at my grandson?" she shrieked. Two skiers with screwdrivers jumped back guiltily.

"Idiots! You broke his skin!" She pointed toward his neck where the trail of pink started.

"What? No way, ma'am. We're not even working over there. We're being careful."

"Get away from him! You could take off his ear or something, and he'd never know!" She advanced on them, poking at them with the walker. They backed off hastily, hands up, eyes on the spikes that gleamed from the rubber pads of the feet.

She jabbed once more, and they ran. She heard the blades of a helicopter overhead. She hoped it was a news crew and that they'd caught her chasing those boys off. Idiots! How oblivious can anyone be?

A screech returned her attention back to her grandson just as a blond girl with a purple blow dryer jerked away from where she'd been melting his arm. The ice had cracked as far as the elbow and he was snatching in her direction, arm wiggling, fingers opening and closing spasmodically. The pole that hung loosely from his hand slipped off.

"Easy!" LinnAnn hobbled over, spiked walker splashing in the slushy snow. She grasped the flailing arm, holding his gloved hand in both of his. "Easy now. We'll get you out."

"Ouuuut." He started coughing and the blunt fell out of his mouth.

"Hey, now! Don't be careless. That's my most expensive blend, you know." He answered with coughs and grunts. He started straining against the snow. Cracks started to form.

"Don't panic, honey. What is it? Are you not getting enough air? Quick, concentrate on his neck and chest! He needs air!"

As if in answer to her pleas, the helicopter moved closer.

Neeta watched in helpless horror as an elderly woman—with a walker, no less!—grabbed hold of the zombie's hand and comforted it. She could see its head straining toward the woman, its mouth opening.

"Tim, you have to warn them. Don't you have a loudspeaker?" she shouted.

"No! I've called the lodge. I told them be subtle, get folks away calmly."

Subtle? Whatever, as long as they're told.

"Kevin is going to tell them to get back to the lodge."

"Kevin?" Mandy's harpy shriek returned. "Kevin's an idiot!"

Altimeter shot back, "He was about ready to announce lunch. He's at the loudspeaker. Do you want this done fast?"

"Just get me in close." Neeta hollered over them both.

Below them, people started running.

Grandma LinnAnn pushed the fat joint back into her grandson's mouth. "Now, you just chomp down on that—but don't bite my finger!" She jerked her hand back, a piece of her glove tearing. "Listen to me, boy. I know you're freaked, but we'll get you free in a minute."

The lodge loudspeaker came on with a computer-generated whine of feedback, causing people to wince. She bit back her irritation. That Altimeter and his need for retro. The person making the announcement cleared his throat and stammered. It was that cafeteria boy, Kevin, probably announcing lunch. Couldn't he wait until they'd saved her grandson?

"Um, excuse me? People by the snowman-person…uh, thing? Listen, so, don't panic or anything 'cause I might lose my job, but you guys really need to back away from that snowman-person-thing."

"His name is Ethan!" LinnAnn hollered.

"Ethan?" Someone repeated and took off running. So did a couple of others.

LinnAnn rolled her eyes. What had her idiot grandson done this time?

Kevin was still stammering. "Because he's not actually a person or alive or anything. That's a zombie. So, you know, back up."

What was he going on about? People around her were looking from the lodge to her grandson to each other. More started to edge away, but a few lingered, unsure. Even so, and more important to her, hair dryers had lowered, blasting warm air at Ethan's legs rather than his chest.

"Seriously, guys, he's dead meat, come back…"

She was never selling that Kevin anything again, even if he did get a doctor's order. "Ignore that bumbling fool!" she cried, but almost overtop her words, one of the nice young men aiming a blow dryer at her grandson's neck gave a shout.

"It's true! He's bit." He pointed at Ethan's ear…or what was left of it.

Ethan and snapped at the man's outstretched hand. The man yelped and jumped back, dropping his blow dryer. It landed at the zombie's feet, the large safety tag on its cord floating in a puddle.

A woman screamed. "Oh, my heck! Blow dryer in the water!"

Suddenly, the crowd that had been milling uncertainly around them bolted into panicked action, running, screaming, and snatching up children as they hurried to the wood steps.

Meanwhile, the automatic failsafes in the blow dryer kicked in and its power snapped off with a zap. A canned voice announced, "Attention: Moisture detected around blow dryer electrical system. This blow dryer is not to be used in bathtubs or showers. Please unplug the dryer at the source before handling. If you have questions, tweet the California State Department of Safety at #helpmydryerzwet or go to helpmydryerzwet.ca.gov."

Zombie Ethan twisted his head around, confused at the fleeing crowd. Then, he caught sight of the blonde, purple dryer still in her hand, and his face twisted into a macabre grin. "Chaaaase!"

He strained against the ice. It cracked around him.

Horror spiked LinnAnn, freezing her momentarily, but anger quickly overcame fear, and she hefted her walker before her like a lion tamer's chair.

"Dammit, the one thing I did like about leaving California was no zombies!"

In the helicopter, Mandy gave voice to the alarm Neeta felt. "Tim! You have to get closer!"

"And land where, woman? There are people running around everywhere."

Brown was right; after the initial exodus away from the zombie, people seemed to have forgotten what they were running from. Some dashed about aimlessly, while a few actually ran back toward the zombie. Neeta thought she saw cell phones in some people's hands, but at least two held ski poles. They ran to the old woman, who had her walker in front of her like she intended to single-handedly fend off the zombie. The camera crew was still filming from a safe distance...for now.

That was Chill Winters reporting. She never backed down from an extreme reporting challenge.

The corpsicle had nearly broken free of its icy prison.

I have to do something! Neeta's stomach flipped because there was only one thing she could do. Didn't she just that morning warn Ted against it?

She pointed at the copilot's helmet. "Give me your helmet! Tim, hover as close as you can. Mandy, I need rope. Sturdy rope."

Mandy's face went pale, but she nodded and leaned forward to dig in the storage bin under her seat. Neeta pulled on the helmet and prayed that she could wait to throw up until after the cameras had stopped filming.

Chapter 13

After a brief argument that ended when she swung her walker at them, Grandma LinnAnn had bullied the two men who'd come to save her into taking positions around the zombie instead. People had stopped screaming but yelled out useless encouragement: "Go for the eyes!" "Take out its knees!" "Get out of the way! I'm filming for the ZomBlog contest!"

The blow dryer at its feet had cycled through its warning in Spanish and was now complaining about water in the nozzle. "To clean this appliance, we recommend B-to-Z appliance wipes. From Bacteria to Zombies, nothing gets the job done like B-to-Z. Learn more at…"

Kevin was stammering over the loudspeaker but seemed to have forgotten what he was trying to say. Idiot boy! What had happened to him? She remembered when he bought his first joint from her. He was such a sharp kid then; only 12 and talking about becoming a geneticist. If she weren't so convinced GMOs led to human and global fattening, she'd have been tempted to ask him about developing some new strains. Now, he couldn't even remember the impending zombie attack.

She wasn't selling him another joint again, even if he was her best customer and had it covered under the Government Mint plan. He was a white male—she didn't need a reason to refuse his patronage.

The helicopter was getting closer, its blades kicking up a breeze and splattering water and snow. Who was that idiot behind the controls, anyway?

The zombie that had been her grandson had freed its torso and one knee and had finally gotten enough sense to hack away at the ice with its fists.

They needed help—real help, not an old woman and two guys with poles. Where was that California exterminator? The one from that show...?

"Neeta Lyffe! I need Lyffe!" LinnAnn hollered. She saw someone run into the lodge and another person start dialing his phone. She hoped it was for her sake. In the meantime, what was that talk show she'd seen with Neeta's mom, Carol? Oh, yeah: Zombies keep the habits they made in life even in death.

"Boy, what do you think you're doing?" She had to yell to be heard over the chopper. "That's my best grass, and you aren't even enjoying it. If you love your Grandma LinnAnn, you'll stay still and take a good puff. Come on, show Granny how you do it French."

"Are you nuts?" one of the guys yelled, but the zombie stopped tearing at the ice around its legs and took a deep drag. Smoke came out of the hole in its neck, but if even with the chopper kicking up a breeze, it managed to get some back into its nose.

"That's right. It pays to recycle!"

The intercom squeaked as Kevin cleared his throat. "Yeah, so, anyway, um, get away from the snowman-person-thing. It's totally a zombie.

They'd like everyone indoors, so we're going to have a sale on our nachos…"

"Naaachos!" Zombie Ethan broke free of ice and shambled toward the snack bar…and Grandma LinnAnn.

"Nachos?" Neeta squawked. "We have a zombie who died toking, and you told them to announce nachos?"

Altimeter replied with asperity. "We had to do something. Who doesn't like nachos? I'm as close as I can get. Wind's picking up. I'll hold as steady as I can."

Mandy stood in front of her, tightening the last buckle on the rescue harness they had in the chopper. "Are you sure you want to do this?"

"Have I got a choice?"

Mandy walked behind her, gave the clip on her back a yank to make sure it was secure, and called to Benjy to open the door.

Cold air blasted her. She welcomed it. It soothed her nausea, and maybe everyone would take her wince as a reaction to the cold and not to fear. Phantom pressure on her calf and arms reminded her that just a few hours ago, she'd been hanging from a ski lift with a mostly intact sham-bler trying to climb up her leg.

Forget that. You've got a job to do. She stepped to the open door and looked down to gauge her descent. Altimeter Brown really was a good pilot; they hovered so that she could descend behind the zombie. It had freed itself of the ice but had tan-gled its feet in an electrical cord. As it kicked about, trying to dislodge the cord, two men poked at it with ski poles, but they made a weak defense. Be-tween the zombie and the snack bar, the old woman stood her ground, her walker before her. Neeta thought she was shouting, but she couldn't hear anything over the chopper.

There were not enough cuss words in the Eng-lish language for this job. To distract herself, she started reciting every profanity she could think of in German—they sounded suitably vicious with the right emphasis, no matter what they meant.

She stepped off the chopper.

✕

Zombie Ethan had gotten his foot caught on the dryer cord, which voiced new protests. "Please unplug at the socket. Pulling at the cord can cause damage that may result in injury or death. For more information, tweet the California Department of Safety using hashtag…"

"Look!" a woman yelled. "Someone's jumping out of the chopper!"

Grandma chanced a look up. No, someone was being lowered out of the helicopter. What kind of idiot? Or was that…

The person activated something in her hand, and a long ray of light emitted from the handle. It wobbled before steadying into a straight blade.

Oh, thank heavens! It was her. It was Neeta Lyffe!

Others realized it, too. People started to jump and cheer. Neeta waved. Really? Hamming it up? Her mother was never like that. She was yelling something, too.

A moan drew LinnAnn's attention back to the zombie. It was almost on her.

She hefted her walker and swung hard.

"Ficken esel bruchbude!" Did those words even make sense together? Neeta stepped out of the chopper. She expected to drop and swing once she was off the chopper floor, but instead, she lowered relatively smoothly. One thing to go right in a huge vacation of wrong. She didn't waste any more breath on swears or thanks but made sure her sword pointed away from herself and her cable before powering it on. The monofilament flopped in the wind caused by the rotors and she had a horrifying moment of fear that it would arch her way and slice her, but as the electric field took hold, it steadied into a straight line. She was going to give Wolfe Swords the best endorsement ever if she survived this!

Meanwhile, the crowd was pointing at her. She could hear the cheers even over the chopper. How stupid were these people? It wasn't a show! She waved her free hand and shouted, "Get inside!"

Then, the zombie freed its leg from the cord and started toward the old woman.

"Ficken kamel knacker! Tim! Get me down there! Lower me faster!"

A rush of wind knocked the chopper just as Neeta was in the middle of another swear word and sent her swinging toward the zombie.

Grandma LinnAnn's legs might have been weak, but hours a day of harvesting and rolling her own had given her a fair amount of arm strength.

Her walker connected with her zombie grandson's jaw with a smack she felt up to her elbows. The joint flew out of his mouth, along with some teeth and a fair amount of his skin. He staggered to the side.

LinnAnn backed away. Her foot slipped on the ice, and she fell hard. Her head smacked against the step. She saw stars, and when her vision cleared, she was looking into the half-torn face of the zombie, and any resemblance to her happy, high grandson was gone.

She raised her walker, but it smacked it from her hands. She gave her last defense one fleeting glance as it slid from her reach. No way could she stand and run, even crawling up the steps would just bring her closer to the zombie's mouth. She went with the only weapon she had. "Boy! Did you lose that joint? Go find it! Go find your joint."

"Munchies," it moaned. "Braaains."

She closed her eyes. What a horrible way to go—and in Storm's Brunt, Utah, no less! She could see the headlines: "Local marijuana dealer eaten to death by zombiefied druggie grandson." Utahans wouldn't understand. If she weren't going to die, she'd die of embarrassment. Well, at least it was family...

Then she heard Neeta Lyffe roaring like a Valkyrie. A buzz and a plop.

She opened her eyes a crack. The zombie lay on its side twitching as it tried to make its body obey its commands. She caught a whiff of burning flesh and saw smoke coming from its back. Neeta must have severed its spine. She opened her eyes fully and pushed up the steps away from it.

Neeta was still swinging lightly, but as LinnAnn watched, she hit a release on her rigging and dropped the last few feet, slipping on the melted but refreezing snow, yet catching her balance before she toppled over. She walked to the struggling zombie, reactivating her sword. With a clean swipe, she cut off its head.

There was a moment of silence save the ever-present chopper. Then the crowd erupted into thunderous cheers.

Neeta leaned forward, bracing her hands against her knees as she caught her breath. A few pants, and she shook herself and fetched the walker. She set it in front of LinnAnn and extended her hand to help her up. "Don't take this in until it'd been decontaminated. That was incredibly brave. Are you all right?"

LinnAnn found herself so shaky and weak, she could barely keep standing even with the walker. Nonetheless, old habits took hold. "Oh, I'll be fine, dearie, but you look stressed. Maybe you could use something to relax you? I take all insurances."

Neeta turned down the woman's offer of "discounted relaxants—high grade," but she had to admit, she was still shaking inside. Zombies be damned, it was the dangling from great heights that would make her quit this job.

She worked off the excess adrenalin helping clean up the site, but decontamination meant she again had to strip and shower outdoors. Even though this time, the lodge provided hot water and a heater blowing into the little tent they set up behind the lodge, she was shivering by the time she finished. Mandy met her outside the tent with a change of clothes from Neeta's room, a blanket, gloves, and some snow boots. They still had the tag.

"Tim wants you in his office ASAP." She handed her the boots like they were a peace offering.

Neeta didn't get her hesitation, but she didn't care. The boots looked warm as well as cute, and they fit perfectly. She put the clothes on over the paper outfit and draped the blanket over her head. In addition to being warmer, it helped hide her identity as they crossed the hangout area, which was filled with worried skiers munching nachos and discussing the zombie snowman. A few had joints, and she thought she caught a whiff of nutmeg in the smoke.

Her phone rang as they entered the hall. Ted. She used her chattering teeth to pull off a glove so she could swipe it to answer. "Babe, are you okay?" she asked.

"Okay? I just saw your rescue on TV. How can I be okay, when I'm here and you're over there doing, doing that?"

His voice was strangled and hoarse. She didn't know if that was good or bad. "Babe, trust me, I would never have done that if I could have avoided it."

"I know—but you did! Do you have any idea how sexy you are? You pegged the hot meter! Maybe it's just as well I'm stuck here because if I could see you now, morphine or not, there'd be no waiting until we're married."

Neeta burst out laughing, but Ted continued, his tone earnest. "I mean it, Boss. I have never been so turned on in my life. I wish I could... Are you alone?"

Something in the way he asked that gave her jelly-legs. "I'm in the elevator. With my sister. The minister. We're heading to Brown's office."

"Call me when you're alone." He hung up.

She pulled her phone away so she could see his icon smiling back at her. She wasn't cold anymore. How could that man get her so hot and bothered with just the promise of a phone call?

They hadn't set a date the other night. Instead they'd gone to her room and made out. The only "plan" they'd settled on was that Roscoe would make a lovely bridesmaid. Ted had been teasing her but when he was kissing her next, she'd agreed to just about anything.

She wanted to agree to everything. If only they could find time to get married!

Mandy leaned toward her, looking at the phone. "Oh, was it Ted? What'd he want? How's he feeling?"

Neeta didn't answer, even though she knew exactly how he felt and what he wanted. She did, too.

What did he say on the drive? "When we make time, Babe. You Lyffe women are too much about business. That has to change now that you're the future Mrs. Lyffe-Hacker." He's right. And it changes now.

"Neeta? Everything okay?"

"Mandy," she asked, "how long does it take to get a marriage license in Utah?"

Mandy squealed and threw her arms around Neeta. This time, Neeta didn't want to protest. She hugged back and even hopped up and down with her half-sister. It was going to happen! She was going to marry Ted!

The doors opened, and Mandy left her to see Altimeter while she made some phone calls to friends she had at the courthouse. "We'll get the license through fast. Don't you worry. This isn't my first quickie wedding!"

Neeta didn't know how to respond to that, so she just gave her a wave and headed to Tim Brown's office, her feet hardly touching the floor.

Brown scowled at her from across his desk, flanked by a nervous lodge manager and a harried event organizer. Captain Lars of Z-Mat leaned against the wall, his arms crossed, his face set in a way she recognized from the mirror. Only his professionalism was keeping him from strangling someone. She hoped it wasn't her. He caught her glance and his mouth twitched in a sympathetic smile. She relaxed just a bit. She needed Z-Mat on her side.

Altimeter harrumphed as if to say it was about time she decided to join them. "I hope you're happy. We have people checking out by the dozens. The only reason my lodge isn't empty is because Z-Mat has us on lockdown until they're sure the scene is secure."

Neeta was liking the Salt Lake Z-Mat more every day. Competent and careful, despite their lack of practical experience. "I didn't bring your zombies in, Altimeter, and my fiancé and I have put ourselves in significant danger to take them out for you."

"What's that catch phrase of yours? Part of the job?"

She resisted the urge to lean over the desk and smack Brown across the face, like she'd promised earlier. It didn't matter that she didn't have a zombie arm to do it with. Her own would feel just as satisfying. "Which you've done your best to limit for fear of spooking your guests."

"Well, you've done an admirable job of that regardless, haven't you?" His voice dripped sarcasm, but before she could snark back, he continued with the attack. "That snowman has been there for days, yet you never thought to check it out unobtrusively."

"I'm from Southern California! Yet I should be suspicious of a snowman that everyone had been playing with for hours?" Nonetheless, her reply held an edge of guilt. That Z-Mat rookie had noticed something off about the snowman. She'd even been about to check when another zombie took their attention, and then Ted—

Ted! Suddenly, the horror of the morning flooded over her, and she felt herself shaking again. "My fiancé nearly died today. We are not skiers. We've never exterminated under these conditions. We have never come across zombies so actively mobile at these temperatures. Zombies usually go dormant in the cold. Nothing about this job is ordinary. I'll be writing a letter to your governor praising your Z-Mat team for the incredible job it's done so far because, without them, a lot of people would probably be dead and turned by now, but don't you dare discount the work Ted and I have done."

Captain Lars chimed in. "It was Ted's idea to set traps, and Neeta's to draw them to us with the cameras, then the ski lifts. We may have done more kills today, but they supplied the tactics and experience. Not to mention, she just jumped out of your helicopter to take out that snowman."

Altimeter closed his eyes as if seeking patience dealing with an obstinate and stupid customer. "None of which negates the fact that the ski contest is tomorrow, we still have one zombie terrorizing my slopes, and the competitors and spectators want to leave."

"But, sir," the manager cut in. "We are getting calls from people wanting to know if we have vacancies and from people wanting to attend the event. Neeta's rescue made national news."

Neeta had had plenty of experience with zombie fans who thought rekilling should be a spectator sport. Wasn't that what drove Dave to create Zombie Death Extreme? For that matter, the ZDE fandom probably accounted for a lot of the hotel's calls.

Altimeter had a gleam in his eye.

Neeta held up her hands to ward off his next thoughts. "You can't bring those people in. Don't turn this into a sideshow."

"I don't think that's your concern any longer. We'll have a check for you at the front desk tomorrow morning for services rendered, but all things considered, you'll probably be more comfortable in a hotel in Ogden, closer to your fiancé."

Her stomach sank. "There're still zombies out there."

"One zombie, I'm told."

"That we know of," the captain chimed in, desperation mixed with anger in his voice. "We're still running missing persons checks and testing the zombie's stomach contents—something she recommended, by the way. Besides, it's Tom Spars. He's going to be impossible to catch. Good as my team is, we need Neeta's help."

"I'm sure you can hire her in some advisory role, but I don't want her on my slopes. Now, if you'll excuse me, I have damage control to attend to." Altimeter turned his back on them, set his tablet on his lap and started talking to Peterson. The event organizer stood blinking helplessly until

Brown snapped his name, and like an assistant app, he started answering questions.

Neeta stormed out of the room, Captain Lars on her heels. He slammed the door hard enough to make the wall shake. "Neeta, consider yourself hired. This isn't done!"

A few minutes later, Neeta's suite door also closed with a satisfying slam. She stormed into Ted's room to pack his things first. Ted! She promised to call him back when she was alone. Of course, Altimeter Brown had to ruin her amorous mood. Still, if anyone could bring it back, it was Ted.

When he didn't answer his cell, she called his room and got the nurse. "He was overexcited by something he was watching, so we gave him a sedative. Would you like to leave a message?"

Neeta was pretty certain she'd hung up before she howled in rage. What else could happen?

The phone rang again: "C is for Choice" by Rainbow over Sesame Street.

She slid her thumb over the screen as she composed her voice into a semblance of calm. "Roscoe, hi. Listen, I'm not in the mood for chit-chat."

"Oh, gawd! No truer words, I'm sure. I saw the news footage on the BO Network. I flipped on just as they'd finished the details, but I saw you on the slopes. I had to wait though a whole diatribe about how this totally proves Global Warming was right all along, but anyway—is it true? It's Slay Bells?"

She put the phone on speaker so she could start packing Ted's stuff. His suitcases were still half full, and the rest of his outfits lay strewn on the floor and dresser. "Most of them are down now, but yeah, that was the team. We've got one left. He's wily."

Roscoe squealed like a crazed fan girl. "Is it Tom Spars? Oh, gawd, of course it is. You couldn't stop that man when he was alive."

"You knew him?" Roscoe may have been one of the contestants on her show, but he'd been a plant, a Hollywood actor who got hired to stir things up, take points from the others, get people to love and hate him, and make a dramatic departure in the finale. As such, he connected with a wide range of people, but skiers?

"Oh, gawd, yes. I'm a big fan of the sport, and let's just say Tom and his wife didn't limit their adventures to the slopes, shall we? But never mind the gossip! Girl, you are not going to catch him by conventional means, not while he's skiing."

The simple act of folding clothes soothed Neeta's nerves, despite the fact that they were going into a suitcase a week early. As her anger cooled, her mind returned to the problem. She wouldn't leave the Z-Mat team to handle this themselves, even if they hadn't just hired her. "Okay. Suggestions for traps? Z-Mat got a couple that way."

"Not Tommy. There's not an obstacle he can't overcome, and if he does fail, he'll rage quit. I do mean rage. I saw him miss a jump once, and he came back around and took it out—like, destroyed, I mean. He threw his poles at the guy that tried to stop him. He even bit the branch off a tree before they could calm him down. It disturbed me, and you know how I feel about passionate expression. If you trap him and miss, it will not be pretty."

"We tried to take them out on the lifts, but he's not riding them."

"He had special skis with some kind of thrust assist. They were amazing. You could ski uphill. They were indestructible—like titanium or something. I remember reading that right after he died, they searched for his skis, you know, in case they came off in the avalanche. Omyheck! You think he still has them—and they're still working?"

Neeta closed Ted's suitcase and walked to the sliding doors to peer out at the slopes. The sun had set so quickly! The moon bathed the snow in a blue light. The lodge had all the lights off to discourage anyone going out. She saw stars, thicker than she'd ever seen before; a wide swath of the Milky Way shone soft like a moth's wing between two trees. It should have taken her breath away, but all she could think about was a zombie on hoverboard skis blasting uphill.

"Maybe. They'd have to be able to take the snow and cold, and if they stayed on his feet… Roscoe, I'm out of my element. Any ideas?"

Roscoe hummed in thought. "He's good, but he's a glory hound. He always had to be first, always the best. Always on top, if you know what I mean. What an ego. Plus, he was such a lech, but he always cleared things with Muchelle. A gentleman, that way. Other guys would be all over the trophy girl, while he was busy mugging it up for the cameras and waving his trophy in everyone's face. But he'd be checking her out, and if he liked what he saw… Oh, girl, there was this one time with this buff blonde… You'd think he hadn't noticed her, but that night in the lodge…"

She thought she saw movement in the distance, but she couldn't tell. Roscoe's gossip became a buzzing in her ears. She cut him off. "Roscoe, you know I can't get him into the lodge! Do you have anything helpful?"

"Sorry, Neeta. That's all I know…but there is something I can give you! It was supposed to be for your wedding shower. Kind of a gag gift, though after San Francisco, I think you'll find it handy. Besides, Ted might like it. I think there's some hidden friskiness in that man."

"Roscoe!" She felt her face heat.

He chuckled. "That's okay. You don't have to tell me, unless you want to. Anyway, it might fit under your ski clothes better than that hazmat suit you have. I'll drone it to you, and you'll have it in the morning."

"Okay." Her eyes strained, and she was starting to get a headache. The last of her adrenalin was burning off. She let the curtain drop. "So, are you going to tell me what it is, or is it a surprise?"

"You can't guess? Transparent Kevlar, of course!"

Neeta chased the zombie down a slope called "Nine Fingers." Her board hovered over a wave of snow, making it operate more like a surfboard. Finally, something she could handle with confidence! The transparent Kevlar suit fit perfectly under the white ski suit the ghost of her biological father gave her as a wedding gown. It kept her warm despite the winds from her impossibly fast pursuit. Even so, Spars stayed stubbornly just ahead of her.

"You can't win!" she screamed at it. "Just rage quit! Bite a tree so I can slice your head off!"

"Dude, are you threatening the environment? Not cool." A tube of moonlit snow opened up beside Neeta. Bergie surfed through. One of his hands skimmed the snow, causing a splash of rainbow slush. The other held his decapitated head before him so that the wind could ruffle his sunbleached hair.

Neeta'd had it. With a shriek of fury, she lifted her knees and twisted, bringing the board down edge first into the snow, perpendicular to the slope. She drew sparks as she slid to a stop, her body facing uphill.

"Sweet!" The tunnel of snow collapsed around Bergie. His board disappeared. He stepped forward lightly as if it had all been planned. "Awesome plant!"

Neeta held her hand away from her body and willed her chainsaw into it. She tabbed it on, letting the roar feed her confidence. "All right, Eidelberg. You have thirty seconds to explain why you are still in my head, messing up my dreams, and it had better be good or I will give you a lobotomy."

"Whoa! Chill. You know that'd be, like, lobotomizing your subconscious, right?"

She revved the chain. "Twenty seconds."

Bergie's face twisted with hurt. "You know, I'm here because you put me here!"

Right. Because she just loved having nightmares about friends she'd had to decapitate. The notion was so ridiculous, she raised the chainsaw in reply.

Bergie hugged his head against his chest. His voice was muffled from his arms. "Okay! Fine! Let me ask a question. Why'd you let me go into a zombiefied area dressed in plastic wrap?"

She lowered the chainsaw in surprise, and it traced the ZDE symbol in the snow. Poppies sprouted from it. She barely noticed. Really? For over a year, he'd haunted her dreams to ask her why she approved his fashion choice?

The memory came back. Standing in front of the makeshift warehouse on the set of Zombie Death Extreme, gaping as Eidelberg stepped out of the van in his homemade Z-Mat suit: A helmet, board shorts, and layers upon layers of plastic wrapped tightly over his fabulous body. "Let's do this thing, baby!" Hearing Dave hoot over her earpiece: "Now, that's how to wow the audience."

"Would you have let Ted go on a rekill like that?"

"Yes! No! I don't know! It was a TV show. There were supposed to be safeties in place." Two zombies. Dave had told her two zombies awaited them in the warehouse. She could take out two on her own, and she had eight armed plebes to assist.

"You let me go in there dressed in plastic wrap."

Telling Dave to stop the show. Dave laughing and saying he had confidence in her. "I put you in the center of everyone, Bergie! All you should have had to worry about was splatter. Now, do you mind? There's a zombie loose. I have people to protect."

"Why didn't you protect me?" Bergie's arms moved his head so he could look her in the eye. "Why didn't you protect me?"

"You were supposed to protect yourself!" she screamed. "That was the whole point of the whole damn show. Learning to be smart with the chances you took. I would never have had to make that decision with Ted. He takes chances, but he's smart about them. I thought you were, too."

Her eyes filled with tears, blurring the vision of the surfer with the severed head. "I wanted to stop the episode. Dave wouldn't let me. I put you in the middle of everyone. You were meat-shielded. You were the safest person in that warehouse, even safer than the cameramen. You jumped out of formation, Bergie! You left the group like I'd warned everyone not to. The zombies were on you before I could snatch you back. I tried to protect you, but I can only do so much against stupid!"

Her word echoed across the mountainside, but instead of causing an avalanche, it froze the snow she'd forgotten was heading her way. The world grew so silent, her ears pounded.

"Wow. You're right." Bergie settled his head on his neck. The torn flesh on both sides reached out like tentacles and interwove until it was secure. "I was totally stupid. So, feel better?"

She stopped to scrub her eyes. "That's it? All this time, you wanted me to tell you, you were stupid?"

His head tilted, pulling at the flaps, but they held. "I think maybe you needed to tell yourself I was stupid. Or maybe this is one of those closure things? You know, like working out Daddy issues?"

She indicated the white ski suit she wore. "I think I might have done that in an earlier dream."

He nodded and pursed his lips. "That's an awful wedding gown."

She rolled her eyes. "I know, right?"

"A tankini with a train. Now, that'd be gnarly. So, like, are we good? Can I, you know, like, come back sometime?"

"With or without your head on straight?" She snickered. It felt so good to laugh, even if it was a macabre joke.

"Whatever shoots your tube, baby."

He lifted his head off his neck like doffing his hat, and it was a moment before she could stop laughing enough to ask, "What about the cryptic messages? In life, you were anything but cryptic."

"That's totally you, baby. Don't shoot up Messenger."

She clutched her sides. "That's an anti-drug slogan, you nut! The idiom is 'Don't shoot the messenger.'"

Bergie gave her a gentle smile. "Laugh more, Neeta Lyffe. You are awesome hot when you laugh."

A small avalanche of snow broke free from the rest and flooded over him, and he was gone. Then, like the Cheshire Cat, his head reappeared. "Hey, speaking of hot. Didn't Roscoe say Spars had the hots for buff blondes who give him trophies? Just a thought. Hope it's not, like, too cryptic or anything."

Neeta sat up in bed. She scrambled for her phone. 4:30 a.m., but she didn't care. She dialed Mandy's number, and when she heard her half-sister's sleepy mumble, said, "Wake up that husband of yours and give him the phone. I know how to catch our zombie."

Chapter 14

Welcome back to Extreme Sports with your Utah correspondent, Chill Winters. This has been the most extreme of extreme competitions, and the contest hasn't even started. And have we got the pre-contest exhibition for you!

Extreme Ski fans will remember the team, Slay Bells, that disappeared while skiing in an avalanche zone. Talk about extreme death! Well, Slay Bells has returned for the comeback of the century. And I do mean come back—as in "come back from the dead." The zombiefied team managed to dig themselves up just in time for the contest and have taken over the slopes. Contest organizers tried to cover it up, but we acquired this footage of an extreme rekill by the Salt Lake City Z-Mat team. Take a look!

See that wire they're stringing across the picnic table? It'll cut through anything. Don't believe me? Watch as Flannelette Sewenge comes in…nice, easy jump, very relaxed. She's just warming up. Do zombies need to do that? The Z-team backs away fast as she hits the table and—Oh! Right through the calves. Slice is nice! The body topples and gets dispatched by Z-Mat member Brook Bridges. Oh, my heck, is that an AX? This woman is extreme! Panning now to the legs. They hit the mogul and fail the 360! Too bad for Flannelette.

All but one of the rest of the Slay Bells team have been similarly dispatched by SLC Z-Mat and the drool-worthy extreme exterminator team of Neeta Lyffe and Ted Hacker. With only World Cup winner Tom Spars left, they're hoping to entice him into the open by letting him compete—and we get to watch.

People, this is extreme danger! But don't worry! The crowd is behind safety glass in case of attack or spoor from his extermination. Of course, Neeta Lyffe herself will do the dispatching.

Oh, and there's Neeta at the bottom of the slope. Doesn't she look amazing? Is she really going to do the re-kill in a tank top and cut offs? That's extreme! People, don't try this at home unless you're auditioning for the Darwin Awards.

Wait. I'm getting a text. Yes! Spars has taken the bait and is in the starting box. Look at him prepping. You'd think after a year under the snow he'd be nervous about his first competitive run, but he's cool as ever. What a professional. A joy to watch, living or undead.

Speaking of cool, joy to watch, and extreme, click on our icon below to see Ted Hacker's extreme footage of the entire team hamming it up for the helicam, right before a hunter spooks them. But do it in another window. Spars is about to make his run!

Transparent Kevlar did not hold in heat.

Neeta hadn't expected Roscoe's gift to be a skin-tight bodysuit, either…although, knowing Roscoe, she should have suspected. With a pair of cut-off shorts she borrowed from Mandy and a Zombie Death Extreme tank-top as the only coverings over it, she felt ridiculous as well as cold. At least her head was warm; she was wearing a helmet with the logos of the motorcycle company sponsoring the contest. She didn't know what bikes and skis had in common, but counted her blessings, anyway. Mandy had glued blond extensions on it to simulate wisps escaping. Neeta's own hair was too short, anyway. She's also done Neeta's make-up. It was flashier than Neeta liked, but it did make her look more like a model hired to hand out trophies than an exterminator hired to take out the undead.

Beside Neeta, a huge trophy sat on a short table. Her sword sat beside it. She wished she could have it hanging on her arm, but they didn't know how Spars would react if he saw it. The helmet was weird enough.

Between Roscoe's gift and her dream, she'd realized that the best way to trap the zombie skier was to make it come to her. Spars had died before finishing the contest.

They would let it run the course, whereupon they'd declare it winner and she—the buff blonde babe—would present it with the trophy. Chill Winters had dug into the Extreme Sports archives to show her video of Spars winning other awards. If his zombiefied self acted true to form, it would give her a once-over, snatch the trophy, and then turn its back on her to shake the trophy at the crowd and crow. She'd grab the sword, drop her face shield down, and take off its head.

Of course, in order to make the charade as convincing as possible, they had to have an audience. Tim found that when his guests were given the choice, more than a few were only too glad to stick around, sign waivers, and watch the spectacle from the bleachers. They'd put up some hasty barriers and plastic shielding in case things didn't go well and got messy. The front row was filled with Z-Mat members. She just hoped that if any deaths got witnessed, it was be limited to hers.

Don't think like that! You're getting married in three days, thanks to Mandy. You can die after the honeymoon!

Ted's voice came over her earpiece. "It's in the box, babe. Get ready. Once it starts, it'll only take a couple of minutes to make it down the slope."

"Good, because I'm freezing. I may never leave SoCal in the winter again."

He chuckled, but she could hear the strain in his voice. He'd insisted on checking out of the hospital to take part of the op. The doctors had resisted until accounting informed them that a coding error had classified him as a routine C-Section, which under the Government Standard policy only warranted an overnight stay. Rather than face two hours of refiling online, they'd given him some painkillers, the mandatory pamphlets on Breast Milk vs. Formula, and sent him on his way. On the bright side, the painkillers allotted for a C-section were superior to those for a chopped-off finger. Unfortunately, they seemed to be wearing off after the trip and the cold.

Nonetheless, he said, "Well, you look amazing. That's a totally sexy outfit. You're going to keep it, aren't you?"

"Roscoe was right," she murmured.

"What?"

"Nothing. Is it ready yet? I'm so done with this job."

"Me, too. We've got wedding guests to invite! Hey, Mom texted. She's met this guy who's a pilot, so maybe... Here it comes!"

Neeta couldn't see the whole course from her vantage point, so she pinned her eyes to just above the highest point while Ted narrated. "It's coming to the jump. Whoa! Triple flip and a twist! This guy's fuze core. Too bad he's dead. Okay, through the slalom flags. See it yet?"

She strained. Nothing. Nothing. There—a figure in fuchsia and turquoise catching big air as it crested the hill. It slammed down in a spray of powder. She thought it had wiped out, but then, there it was halfway down the next hill. "It's fast! Ted!"

"Get ready! Smile!"

The course took it behind the last hill, then another jump. No wonder they couldn't catch it. What if it was going too fast to stop? She pasted on a smile but edged closer to the table.

It came to a sudden stop only a foot from Neeta, sending up a spray that splattered her to her chest.

She shrieked. "Scheibe! That's cold!" She brushed the snow off her shirt.

"Babe, smile. Act like it's funny!" Ted warned.

"Funny?"

Spars, however, was looking from her to the audience, who, now that it stood mere feet from them, no longer saw it as a skier, but a monster. A year of freezing followed by two days to thaw had not done its features any grace. One side of its face had flattened, while the other swelled and discolored. Somewhere along the line, it must have hit a tree; the skin tore away to reveal its teeth to the molars.

What got Neeta, however, were the eyes. Dead eyes should not show so much vexation.

Neeta laughed in what she hoped sounded vapid and beguiling, and did her best game show girl pose, pointing to the scoreboard. "Ted, get that score up there!" she said through grin-gritted teeth.

"It is. Our corpsicle's not looking. Plan B, babe."

Dropping her façade, she reached for her sword. Her hand hit a pile of snow.

Spars let out a roar and swung its ski pole at her.

"I knew I should have held onto that sword!" Neeta yelled as she threw herself over the table and rolled behind it.

She didn't see her sword. Had it fallen in the show? She grabbed the trophy to use as a shield. Over her earpiece, she could hear Ted calling out hasty instructions to the Z-Mat team, but she couldn't pause to see how they were responding.

Spars, true to its temper in life and lacking higher brain functions to remind it that homicide was not good form while being filmed for TV, was having a full-blown zombie meltdown. Roaring, it raised both poles and slammed them down toward her. She raised the trophy to block them.

The cold plastic of the trophy cracked with a sharp retort. The impact jarred her muscles, but she didn't waste any time. Thanking Altimeter for being a cheap giftzwerg, she pressed the two halves of the trophy against the poles and yanked hard. She felt resistance, and then they came free. So did its right hand.

"Yipe!" She ducked her head as the torn flesh flew over her, just in time for the infested flesh to strike her scarf and not her skin.

"Babe!" Ted yelled.

"I know!" She threw herself back on the snow and used her legs to upend the table in Spar's direction. Her sword was lost to her now, but at least she could slam down her face shield. She threw the broken trophy at the zombie. It deflected it easily, but the jagged edge caught one sleeve. Howling with rage, it slapped at it with his handless arm.

That gave Neeta enough time to fling off the scarf and snatch the poles. She flicked the hand off of the one, and held them like dual short swords—thin, weak swords with a bend in the middle and a basket on the end, but anything was a weapon in a pinch. Never taking her eyes off the corpsicle, she stepped upslope, away from the audience, hoping to buy time until the Z-Mat members in the audience slapped on their helmets and got to her. With any luck, she could maneuver Spars so its back was to them for a nice easy decapitation.

The zombie pulled off the trophy, ripping its sleeve. It waved the torn fabric in her direction. "Paaaaay!"

It pushed off with its skis and rushed her.

No way could she run in time. She braced herself and held the poles firmly before her, one in front of her chest, one over her head at face height to it. Time to test the metal, and she already knew hers. Would the metal of the poles match?

Spars never slowed. The first pole struck its chest and sank in to the basket. The other jammed into its mouth.

Neeta twisted hard, shoving Spars to her side before it hit her. Its skis smashed her shins. She flung herself away, but the poles were torn from her hands. One of the zombie's skis popped off. The other snapped. Even titanium had its limits, apparently.

She scrambled to her feet. Where the hell was that Z-Mat team? She chanced a look toward the stands. The Z-Mat team was out in front of the stands, holding back a crowd of spectators brandishing cell phones or ski poles. Idiots. Didn't they have the sense to be afraid?

In front of them, a clothing line logo was emblazoned on the pop-up fence. No Fear. Figures.

She couldn't go back that way for help, not with all those civilians.

Both embedded poles had snapped when Spars hit the ground. It had rolled onto its back and removed the one from its chest, but kept pulling at the pole whose basket had lodged itself in his mouth. Still, she didn't trust it to forget its mission. It could still grab her if she got close enough to snatch the other pole.

"Ted! I need backup!" she hollered into the mike. She heard crackles in reply. "Ted?"

The zombie dislodged the pole, taking most of its teeth with it. Holding it like a club, it rose and hobbled toward her. She ran up the hill. Her boots sunk into the powder, slowing her and making her legs burn with each step, but she jogged on the beach just for this reason. If sand couldn't slow her, neither would snow. The broken ski on the zombie's foot hobbled it. She managed to get a small lead on it by the time she hit the nearest slalom flag.

She stopped and tried to yank it out. Whether it was permanently set or the alternating warmth and cold had encased it in ice, she didn't know, but it stuck tight. She gave it one last yank as she heard a growl. Spars had caught up to her. Without a better idea, she bent the pole back as far as it would go. When the zombie was almost on her, she let them go.

Thwack! The flagpole rebounded, smacking it directly on the face. The zombie bent backward at the knees and started sliding back down the hill on its single ski. She could not make out what it howled, but she got the idea it enjoyed the trip.

She didn't care. It had dropped the broken pole. She snatched it up and ran downhill, trying to outpace it but staying wide of its trail in case she slipped. The last thing she wanted to do was fall in zombie spoor three days before her wedding!

Panting and sweating under her Kevlar, she caught up just as it slammed into the upended picnic table. While it struggled to get its bearings, she raised the pole and jammed the broken end into its hand, pushing as hard as she could to pin it to the base under the powder. It thrashed and struggled, but without its other hand to grip and both its feet pinned under itself, it couldn't gain purchase. She had it stuck, but not for long. What she wouldn't give for her sword—or an ax!

"Brook!"

Suddenly, Captain Lars was beside her. He pointed his gun at the zombie's head. Double-tap. The sharp cracks made her wince, but the zombie stilled, its brain matter leaking into the snow behind its head.

"Twenty-twenty hindsight, we probably should have given you a gun." He gave her an apologetic smile. Gradually, she realized the crowd was cheering.

"I don't know how to shoot…but I'd love to learn." Exhausted, her legs protesting the climb and run, she hobbled to the edge of the table and leaned against it. "Ted, babe, can you hear me? 'Cause I think the headset's broken."

Lars pulled his phone out of his pocket, snickered at the text, and handed it to her. It was from Ted: Boss. You. Are. So. Hot!!!!!! <<<333

Altimeter griped about postponing the contest yet one more day in order to decontaminate the slopes, but Neeta and Captain Lars stood firm. Peterson comforted him with news that the Ute2 HotDogger Competition was making the Extreme Sports Channel's "Top Ten Most Extreme Events of the Year," guaranteeing next year's event would be even more popular. The weather did its best to mollify him as well, with a huge snowstorm that dropped 18 inches of powder the night after the cleaning, then cleared into a perfect day. The publicity of Neeta's battle against Spars drew in record crowds, both for the competition and the special event afterwards.

Peterson wanted them to hold the wedding outdoors to accommodate the spectators, and Mandy waxed poetic about the mountain view backdrop making the perfect temple, but Neeta was done with cold. Instead, the lodge staff filled the great hall with folding chairs draped with white fabric and blue ribbons, and the TV screens from the contest would broadcast the nuptials so interested visitors could watch from stadium seating outside.

Ted's mom's new friend was not only a pilot but owned a small charter company; he commandeered his biggest plane to ferry their most important guests in a day early, just enough time for Neeta and Min to go dress shopping. Remembering her dream, she chose something as far from snowsuit as possible. She felt like a princess walking down the curved staircase in an elegant gown of silk with short sleeves. Jason walked her down the aisle, and even Roscoe had flown in and was dabbing his eyes as he blew kisses to both her and Ted.

Mandy gave a nice opening commentary about how Neeta had surprised her. "Neeta never knew our father, and I'd always pitied her for that. I expected her to be damaged somehow, unable to form relationships because she never had a father's love. Instead, I discovered my half-sister was a beautiful, confident woman, strong physically and emotionally. She's surrounded by friends who are her family—and she chose the most perfect man for her to make a new family with."

They said the Exterminator's Vows. "I take you, Ted, as my husband, in sickness and in health, for richer or poorer, until death do us part; and should undeath bring you back to me, I vow to return you to the peace of the grave." The words were even more poignant to her as she carefully slipped his wedding ring onto the third finger of his damaged hand.

When Mandy pronounced them husband and wife and they kissed, they could hear cheering from the crowd outside.

Even though Neeta had finally gotten used to the idea that she was a celebrity, posing with Ted while news crews snapped their pics and called out questions made her feel self-conscious regardless of Mandy's glowing words about her confidence. Still, she was too happy to care. Today, she was Mrs. Lyffe-Hacker, and nothing could wreck that.

From Ted's pocket, their phones started squawking, "Neeta! 9-1-1!" "Ted! 9-1-1!"

Giving her a confused look, Ted, pulled out the phones. Unearthed graves had been discovered at a cemetery near the LA BottomsUpDome, where a political rally was planned that evening. The attached text said the governor had a helicopter waiting to ferry them. No zombies had been found, but he didn't want to take any chances.

"9-1-1 for a potential outbreak?" Neeta clenched her fists against the urge to text words that would not look so good in print. She didn't think she could spell the German, anyway.

Ted took her phone and swiped it to send a "Not Available" message. "We can go rekill things another day. We deserve a vacation."

"And a honeymoon!"

He stuck the phones into his pocket. "Definitely a honeymoon! You and me."

She wrapped her arms around him, "A couple of boards by day."

His eyes sparkled, "Romantic fire by night."

They chorused: "And no zombies!"

They   kissed   on   it.

Neeta Lyffe and the Best Career Day Ever

The zombie lurched forward, its arms flailing, the strobing lights adding to the jerkiness of its motions. Neeta swung her chainsaw in a cross-block, scoring on its hands, then stepped left to take off its head just as another zombie flung itself on the ground, reaching for her knees. She stomped on the head, using the height advantage to connect with the other across the cranium. Over the roar of her chainsaw, They Mite B Robots screamed musically about re-killing the dead. Neeta joined in the chorus as groaning corpses lurched, swung, and jerked toward her.

Suddenly, the music cut off. The lights brightened, and the simulated undead halted and flopped.

"Hey!" Neeta yelled as she cut off the power to her chainsaw.

"Sorry, Babe!" Ted called from the doorway. "Amanda's principal is on the phone."

"What?" She weaved between the animated dummies and past the treadmill and weights machine, and set her chainsaw on the shelf. She hated leaving the tool with a dye-encrusted guard on, but Mrs. Peabody would consider any delay rudeness—and it "did not do" to be rude to Mrs. Peabody.

Ted handed her a washcloth, then a towel. "You've got a little…" He brushed some simulated entrails off her shirt. She couldn't help but smile; even after eight years, his touch gave her happy shivers.

She fluffed her hair as they headed to the office. "Did she say what she wants?"

"Nah, but she's got the pinched look." Ted made a face, like he'd snorted rather than swallowed a lemon.

Neeta laughed, then whacked him. "Don't let Mandy see you do that."

Mrs. Peabody did indeed have a pinched look, though not to Ted's extreme, which made sense. Mrs. Peabody would never inhale. "Missus Lyffe, so sorry to interrupt your workout. It's commendable that you take fitness so seriously."

Neeta shrugged as Ted pulled up a second chair and sat beside her. "It's part of the job. Is there something wrong? Did Amanda—"

Mrs. Peabody waved her hands as if brushing away butterflies. "Oh, no. Of course not. Amanda is a most gentle soul." Despite her words, she looked accusingly at Neeta and Ted, as if wondering how it was possible.

"That'd be from my mother," Ted declared proudly.

Neeta glanced at him. Last month, his mother beat a burglar senseless with her cane when he broke into her home.

"She crochets doilies. It's a lost art," Ted continued amicably.

The answer seemed to satisfy the principal. "Ah, I see! Well, as I said, it's not because of Amanda that I'm calling, but rather… You know that Career Day is coming up?"

Neeta smiled. A personal invitation? Maybe they weren't so blacklisted after all. "Absolutely! We signed up."

Now the pinch became a grimace. "That's just it. You see, our mission here at Happy Smiles Academy is to foster an environment that protects the innocence of our children against a world that has lost its own."

"Which is one of the reasons we chose Happy Smiles."

"And because you can drink out of the trash cans." Ted added.

"He means they're that clean!" Neeta hastened to explain as Mrs. Peabody's expression twisted from pinched to horrified. "As exterminators, we appreciate a sanitary environment."

Off camera, Neeta reached down with her fist and thumped Ted on his leg.

"Ah, yes, of course. We're not quite to our usual standards since Mr. Carson died. He so loved a tidy school, and we've been hard pressed to train the janitorial staff to his standards."

"I completely understand," Neeta said.

She and Ted shared a grin. They'd met when she was training apprentice exterminators for a reality TV show. Ted hadn't even been a contestant, but he ended up her partner—in more ways than one.

"Oh, well, then! You surely understand our dilemma. While I have the utmost admiration for your work, I feel compelled to ask you to take a…delicate approach…in explaining it to our children."

Neeta burst out laughing. "Mrs. Peabody! I assure you, I have no intention of making a live demonstration."

The principal relaxed.

"In fact, I was thinking of bringing Mandy's flannelgram to illustrate."

"Mandy's grandmother made it!" Ted chimed in. "You'll get a kick out of how the little zombies' heads fall off. Poik!"

Mrs. Peabody's face fell, then pinched again. She straightened in her seat. "Oh, dear. It seems you do not understand our intent. I shall have to be blunt. We'd prefer you limit your presentation to the less emotionally distressing vermin. You may speak briefly about spraying for cockroaches, ants… No furry mammals, please. We must ask that you do not bring your more…crude instruments such as your chainsaw or flamethrower—and under no circumstances should you mention the Z-word." She leaned toward the computer to whisper the last.

"Zombies?" Ted asked.

"Quite."

Ted though a moment. "Can we say 'shamblers'?"

"No, please. That's so offensive to those with ambulatory challenges."

"Corpsesickle?"

"No! Please. I'm sorry, but there's no polite way to refer to the imperfectly resurrected."

Neeta winced. Mrs. Peabody just had to give her husband that challenge. This would not end well.

The principal misinterpreted her expression and gave a little gasp of chagrin. "Oh, my goodness. I'm so sorry! I didn't realize you were religious."

"ARM!" Ted called out. "How about 'ARM'?"

The principal blinked. "'Arm'?"

Neeta swung her foot to kick her husband, but she was too slow.

"Ambulatory Rotting Meat, of course!"

Mandy tossed her backpack into the car and climbed in after it, twisting into the seat and yanking the seat belt into place with a huge sigh. Instead of her usual school uniform, she wore a light blue jumpsuit with the logo for "Lyffe Undeath Exterminations."

"Worst career day ever!" she declared.

From the driver's seat, Neeta turned to smile. She wore a similar version of the jumpsuit, actual protective gear she wore when spraying, although not when re-killing zombies. Mrs. Peabody had made it quite clear that her zombie-fighting suit was inappropriate. Neeta hoped the logo of a woman holding a zombie head while stepping on a cockroach wasn't going to be too much for Mrs.

Peabody, but it was splashed all over the city, and she wasn't going to hide it from the kids.

"Oh, honey. They'll be other career days. You dad can come then."

Mandy pouted. "At least Mrs. Peabody could have let you use the flannelgram. It's so funny when you knock their heads off. Poik!" She made a flicking motion with her fingers.

Neeta sighed and put the car into gear. "Please don't sulk, dear. It's bad enough your dad was moping about not getting to show off his flamethrower."

By the time Neeta had pulled into the parking lot, in a space marked "Reserved for Pleasant Parents," Mandy had brushed off her dark mood and was asking if she could take her father's place in the demonstration. "I can pretend to spray Mrs. Muldoon's desk for roaches!"

"All right," Neeta laughed. "The tank's empty; you can probably carry it on your back."

Neeta pulled the empty tank out of the trunk and made sure the nozzle was properly secured on the side. The thin tube with the rifle trigger was almost as long as Mandy was tall, and the tank as wide, but it didn't stop her daughter from shrugging on the straps and marching it proudly to the office.

"I'm Amanda Hacker Lyffe, and this is my mother, Neeta Hacker Lyffe," she spoke carefully to the security machine as Neeta pressed her thumb against the sensor. The computer bid her welcome and spat out a "Pleasant Parent" badge for her to pin to her outfit.

As they made their way to her room, Neeta glanced into another classroom and saw a teacher replacing a bag in one of the clear Lucite trash cans. She stifled a laugh. Ted did have a point; even the trash cans were immaculate.

Mrs. Muldoon greeted her at the door, and asked her and Mandy to stand by the window while they took attendance and recited the Pledge of Allegiance and sang the Happy Smiles Anthem:

"Happy Smiles Academy!
Being kind to you and me!
When we are good citizens
Our families, country, and world wins!
Happy Smiles Academy
We'll be nice to honor thee!"

In the middle of the song, Mrs. Peabody slipped into the classroom. She beamed at the children, clapping with large, flat hands as they sang. After they finished, she took a spot in the comfy chair at the back of the room and gave Neeta a little princess wave as Mrs. Muldoon introduced her.

Neeta smiled at the class. "Good morning, everyone. As Mrs. Muldoon said, I'm Mrs. Lyffe, and I'm an exterminator. Does anyone know what an exterminator does?"

A boy in the back with a missing tooth and red hair raised his hand high, and she pointed to him. He stood beside his desk.

"Timmy Neidemeyer, ma'am. You whack the heads off corpsicles with your chainsaw. RRR-ROWR!" He made a sweeping motion with his hands.

Some of the kids snickered, but Mrs. Peabody caught Neeta's eye and made butterfly-shooing motions with her hands.

"Well, yes, I do that sometimes," Neeta replied. She wasn't going to lie, after all. "But that's not what I usually do. Most of the time I go after smaller things."

"Zombie squirrels?"

Some of the class giggled.

Mrs. Peabody cleared her throat and, checking that the children were not looking her way, glared daggers at Neeta.

"Squirrels don't become zombies, Timmy. Most of the time, I'm protecting houses from insects like cockroaches—"

"Zombie cockroaches?"

More giggles.

Neeta decided to ignore him. "...and ants and termites. The thing is, sometimes it doesn't matter how clean your home is, you can still get—"

"Janitor zombie!" Timmy declared.

"Mr. Timothy Neidemeyer!" Both his teacher and principal scolded.

But Neeta took in how he stared out the window, gaping and wide-eyed. She ran to the window and looked out just in time to see a leg drag around the corner, leaving a trail of dirt and decay in its wake.

She turned back to Mrs. Peabody. "Lock the school down, now!"

"What? I don't understand."

Neeta was already calling home. "Ted, get over here now, bring the van and the flamethrower!"

"Woooo!"

"Ted! We've got a dead one! Hurry, babe!" She stuffed the phone in her pocket and scanned the classroom.

Mandy was already climbing the cabinet despite her teacher's protests. She pulled down the window cleaner and the dry-erase board spray and tossed them to her mother.

"Good girl!" She shoved the cleaning sprays at Mrs. Muldoon. "Lock the door after me. Keep away from the windows. If something undead gets in, spray it with this."

"What are you talking about?" Mrs. Peabody snarled.

Somewhere in another classroom, children screamed.

Neeta grabbed her spray tank from Mandy then took Mrs. Peabody's arm with the other. "There's a zombie circling the school. Call the office and lock the school down. Do you have zombie protocols? Good—enact them."

She headed for the door.

"Where are you going?"

She glanced back. "To do my job."

She dashed out.

In the hallway, she paused to listen. The screams had stopped. The hallway was silent. Where was it? There'd be more screams if the zombie were in a classroom. And what was she going to do? Beat it with an empty tank? She needed a plan.

"Mom."

Neeta whirled. "Mandy! Get in the classroom."

Mandy set her legs firmly on the floor and crossed her arms stubbornly. "No. I'm going to help you! It'll take Dad ten minutes to get here. That's too long. Teams of two."

"Mandy! You're too young! I'll just hold him off. Get in the classroom!" She grabbed Mandy with one arm and the doorknob with another.

"But you always say teams of two!"

The doorknob clicked locked.

"No!" Neeta grabbed at the knob. She banged on the door. On the other side, Mrs. Muldoon looked from her to Mandy, and her mouth opened in a soundless gasp.

"Attention, Happy Smiles Students!" Mrs. Peabody's automated voice came cheerily over the intercom. "We're having a *little* zombie situation right now. The school is locked down. Please stay calm in your rooms. Teachers, please grab the nearest spray cleaner. Remember: Cleaning products repel zombies! Let's sing the Happy Smiles Anthem while we wait for 9-1-1!"

As Mrs. Peabody began singing the school's adaption of the ABCs, Neeta turned back to the hallway, suppressing a scream. She held Mandy's hand tightly. "Stay close to me, but if I tell you run, you run," she said.

A rattling at the door at the end of the hallway made her sigh with relief. "Okay, he's outside. We have time—"

"Mommy. Timmy said janitor zombie. It's Mister Carson."

"Oh, baby. I'm sorry."

"No, Mommy, they said they buried him with his keys."

Together they stared as the door stopped shaking. Neeta turned and ran in the other direction. "Let's go!"

Ten steps later, Mandy stopped. "Mom, here! Closet!"

Thankfully, the door had been left ajar. Neeta jerked it open and saw the racks of cleaning supplies. Bottles of chlorine bleach, mops, brooms, a mechanical floor waxer, neat stacks of trash cans.

She set her spray can on the floor near the bottles of bleach and unscrewed the top. "Smart girl! Mandy, I need you to fill this as fast as you can, got it? At least half full! Bleach only. Don't breathe the fumes!"

Mandy ran to the bottles and twisted off the childproof caps with difficulty. "Can we hold it off?"

Neeta was digging through the supplies. She found rubber gloves and yanked them on, poured a bottle of TidyToidy over her outfit, then one over her daughter. She grabbed a spray bottle. Empty. Another. Empty.

Behind the last bottle, she found a name plate: Mr. Jonas Carson, Executive Manager, Sanitation.

By now they could hear the moaning of Mr. Carson's reanimated corpse as it shambled its way to the closet.

Her face. She had to protect her face. It only took the tiniest amount of zombie spoor to infect the living. She grabbed a trash can and shoved it on her head.

"If I yell, 'weapon,' toss me something, anything!" Her voice was muffled and she knew she looked ridiculous, but at least she was protected. And it was clean. She grinned as Mandy grabbed a trash can for herself.

She snagged a gallon bottle of window cleaner and dashed out.

A squeal escaped her throat as she cleared the door and nearly came face to face with the rotter. Mr. Carson's corpse was faster than she thought. She poured the cleaner in a protective line before her then splashed the rest its way. It jerked as if stung but continued forward.

Idiot! He was a janitor! He probably loved ammonia.

"Weapon!"

Mandy tossed a plunger at her.

Neeta scooped it up and with a roar shoved it, rubber bell first, at the zombie's face.

It stuck.

She shoved the zombie back, and it stumbled, but didn't lose its balance. It grabbed the plunger with both hands, but instead of pulling it off, began the move the handle back and forth as it swayed side to side. Squelching sounds came from its face.

"Weapon!"

A mop slid to her feet.

She grabbed it and swung. She'd hoped to knock its head off, but it rocked back as it swayed, and the mop impacted the handle of the plunger. With a meaty rip, the plunger pulled away from its face—taking most of its face with it.

It turned to Neeta, and she marveled at how outraged a skinless skull could look. It grabbed the mop and yanked it out of her hands. She backed toward the closet, ready to run head down and batter it away from her daughter if need be.

But it simply took the mop and started pushing the spilled cleaner toward the mess of its own face.

"Weapon!"

Mandy tossed her a broom.

"Bigger next time!" Neeta twirled it in her hands, checking the balance of the broom head, deciding her strategy.

"Sorry! Almost done!" Mandy called.

With the broom head pointing in front of her, Neeta approached, more cautiously this time. Corpsicle Carson remained intent on trying to wipe up a piece of its cheek that had escaped the plunger. She swung low. If she could get enough force to cut off its legs—

At the last minute, it lost its balance, the mop slipped, connected with Neeta's broom.

With a roar of frustration, Neeta spun the broom until it tangled with the mop. The zombie's arms twisted.

Snap!

She may have lost the broom, but at least she had disarmed it. Literally.

It glared at its dismembered limbs, then let out a roar.

Neeta scrambled back. "Weapon!"

"Here!" Mandy grunted and shoved the floor waxer out. It was plugged in.

Neeta turned it on. It shook and vibrated under her hands.

"Here, boy!" she yelled and shoved it at the corpse with all her strength.

But the zombie just twisted its body so that rather than getting knocked over, it spun the machine so that the handles faced it. Then it leaned forward, controlling it with its armless body.

Neeta gaped. "How long was this guy a janitor?"

"Timmy called him neat freak. Timmy said he was born scrubbing floors." Mandy answered. "Mommy, I'm done!"

Neeta checked to make sure zombie Carson was intent on wiping up the rotting flesh mess on the floor, and dashed to the closet. Mandy had even screwed the cap back on.

"Mommy's good girl!" Neeta said. She grabbed the tank and primed the hose as she walked out. She clicked on the turbo button a colleague had created for just such occasions.

The zombie that was once the school janitor had pushed his feet under the waxer, its whole body shaking from the vibration of the machine, causing bits of flesh to fly off its body.

Neeta lined herself up, pointed the hose before her and ran.

As she reached it, she stepped onto the waxing machine to get a better angle and shoved the nozzle of her sprayer down its throat, pressing the trigger.

Seven gallons of bleach fired into the corpsicle's body at high pressure until it leaked out of various holes.

The zombie jerked once, then sank to the ground.

Neeta dumped the tank and backed away, trying not to breathe the stench of decay and bleach. "Now that's extermination!" she said.

"Yay, Mommy!" Mandy squealed from the door.

"Stay there! It's contaminated!" Neeta yelled. She looked herself over, then checked the area around her. Spilled bleach, some arms, a smear of a face. A small spattering of flesh and blood in a small area. Surprisingly little on herself.

"Wow. You really were a neat freak," Neeta said. Just then, she heard the hammering of footsteps. She and Mandy both turned to see Ted dashing down the hall, closely followed by the Los Angeles Z-Mat team.

Ted ran full-out, his flamethrower at the ready, but when he saw them, he skidded to a stop and started laughing. He pointed at her, at his head, at her, and buckled over in mirth.

"I'm never going without my Z-Mat gear again!" Neeta snarled, then started laughing, too.

"Daddy!" Mandy ran and jumped into his arms. "I helped! I helped. Teams of two!"

Ted hugged her hard. "That's my girl! Tough like your mom!"

Neeta sat on the back bumper of her HumVan, clean and dressed in spare clothes. The Z-Mat officers were stowing their supplies and piling the barrel containing the remains of the former Mr. Carson into the truck for disposal. They'd taken her uniform, socks and sneakers as well. She'd liked those sneakers.

Over by a tree, the school counselor talked to a large group of children while in the playground, Ted was showing some of the kids his flamethrower. Several of them had trash cans on their heads. Mandy hung by her father's side, adoring as always. Innocent even when innocence was gone. Neeta blinked back tears.

A delicate throat-clearing interrupted the moment.

"Mrs. Peabody." Neeta stood and offered her hand.

The principal shrank back.

"Don't worry. I'm decontaminated." Nonetheless, she lowered her hand.

"Yes. Of course. I… The kind officers said you could have been killed."

Neeta shrugged. "Zombie-ism is touch-contagious. I was definitely not outfitted for the job. Still, I'm good at what I do."

"Yes. So we saw. That was quite a…creative solution."

Neeta shrugged. "I've known others who have done more with less."

"And Amanda. I'm quite surprised. I wonder that you didn't find our school environment somewhat…tame…"

Neeta shook her head. "Mrs. Peabody. My mother couldn't afford a nice school like this. I went to public school in Chinatown and spent the days running around the back streets with my friends. I can't hide the reality of our work from Mandy, but I can ask that she have a place where she can be a sweet innocent for just a while longer."

Mrs. Peabody smiled the most genuine smile Neeta had seen on her. "I completely understand, and honor that. Of course, Amanda is welcome at our school for as long as you want her here."

Then her face pinched. "However, I'm afraid I must ask one teensy favor…"

"We're banned from the school?" Ted shouted. He paced in front of the living room couch.

"She thinks we traumatized the kids," Neeta said. It was like her mother said. No matter how good a job you do, there will be people who won't appreciate you.

"Us? How about Corpsicle Carson?" Ted raged.

Neeta shrugged. "It's not the school's fault. LAPD is checking to see why his spine wasn't properly severed. We might have just prevented a lot more risings."

"Yeah, I know." He sat down on the couch beside her, and she leaned into his shoulder. "It's a win. And I know I was laughing, but you! You never cease to amaze me."

They were kissing when Mandy burst through the door.

"Best bus ride ever!" she declared and jumped between them. She untangled herself from their hugs and dug through her backpack. "Look, Mommy! These are for you."

They were thank-you notes and drawings of her fighting the zombie. Timmy's was especially splattered in red paint. Below several were the words, "I want to be an exterminator!"

"Best career day ever!" Mandy said.

Bonus Content

I had a bunch of other stuff included in the original version, which was funny (or at least I thought was funny) but in the end, took away from the main story instead of adding to it. I offer it here for kicks and giggles. Enjoy.

A Zombie by Any Other Name

Walking Dead has well over a dozen great euphemisms for zombies. They include Biters, Cold Bodies, Creepers, Lamebrains, Rotters, Roamers and even—don't be insulted—Geek. In fact, people in the story seem to have forgotten the word "zombie" was a legitimate part of our vocabulary.

As often happens in our modern world, real life follows fiction, then gets to the point where it's less believable. In 2019, after the public finally accepted that there was an honest-and-for-true zombie problem, people brushed off those Walking Dead comics, searched up the show, and started using the vocabulary. "Geek" quickly left, as it was not only insulting to the reigning majority of wealthy Americans, but also because the not-so wealthy geeks had started to organize into street gangs and didn't take kindly to "their" term being absconded with. However, those Walking Dead terms and more started floating into the vernacular.

Of course, there are those who prefer Twilight to Dracula—or in this case, Warm Bodies to Walking Dead. The Zombies Are People, Too movement fought on a political and social level to legitimize the shambling dead—or in their terms, the "mortality challenged," and along with trying to reunite families and secure voting rights, they worked to introduce vocabulary more suited to the rotters' "alternate unlifestyle."

Of course, it was all fun and games until someone lost an eye, and in this case, eyes started getting lost because the biters were gouging them out of people for appetizers. It took years of campaigning by people like Carol Lyffe, Neeta's mother, to convince the world that the zombies were indeed creepers, biters, shamblers, and—again, no offense to the PhDs who lost 90 percent of their IQs when they died and came back—lamebrains.

Nowadays, people have reverted back to the word "zombie," although there are still some who prefer "imperfectly resurrected" because it's more sensitive. However, zombie exterminators have kept the colorful vocabulary. It adds levity to the job, and when you alternate between spraying for roaches and putting your life on the line taking out Ambulatory Rotting Meat (ARMs), humor is important for keeping your sanity.

Zombie Death Extreme

The Zombie Exterminator: that new breed of unsung heroes of the 2040s. Who are these people? Where did they learn to wield a chainsaw with such deadly efficiency? More importantly, what kind of person is it that takes on the undead for pay?

Zombie Death Extreme takes you first-hand into the rigorous training of the zombie exterminator. Follow twelve apprentices as a Master Exterminator puts them through the rigorous physical, mental and psychological training for their licenses to rekill. This no-holds-barred reality TV series pits our plebes against themselves, against each other, and against the shambling undead. Who will win the million? Who will survive long enough to get their certification?

Season One—LA: In this exciting first season of ZDE, Master Exterminator Neeta Lyffe of Lyffe Undeath Exterminations trains exterminator wannabes from across the United States and even the Middle East. Country boys, ex-Marines, and beauty queens—all want to test their mettle against the shambling undead. Even Roscoe—third-runner up of Mani-Pedi and three-time Academy Award winner for best Reality TV Plant, trades in his cuticle scissors for a chain saw. In an unexpected grand finale, the plebes rush in to protect the people of Burbank against the greatest infestation in a decade.

Rather tragically, one plebe, Donald "Bergie" Eidelberg, was critically bitten and had to be re-killed during one of the challenges. All things considered, plastic wrap is not a cheap alternative to transparent Kevlar after all. On the bright side, it was an important lesson in zombie defense, and that episode has achieved #5 on Buzzfeed's Most Horrific Videos to Go Viral.

Season Two—Bayou: ZDE heads south as Cajun exterminator Reese LeFountaine takes a new set of trainees under his wing. His way is a lot more structured than Neeta Lyffe's free-wheeling do-or-die, but the danger is no less real. It's alligator hunting, voodoo queens and jazz as this set of plebes takes on the shambling undead of Louisiana.

Real People. Real Zombies. Real Death. Discover what it truly means to be a zombie exterminator in this series iTV calls, "More real than reality TV, more dramatic than drama, more docu than documentaries. It's just more, people!"

Disclaimer: As per the Reality TV Indemnifications Act of 2022, all contestants have certified that they understand that Zombie Death

Extreme is a true-to-life reality TV show. While all reasonable safety precautions (which do not interfere with the drama of the show) are in place, that they are putting their lives on the line for education, duty, and the chance at a million dollars. They do not hold the producers of ZDE or RealDealTV responsible for any physical injury, mental trauma or death.

Warning: This show is rated PG-13 for violence/gore, language, zombie-related mutilations, and tobacco use.

This Week on Big Winners and Big Losers: Marcel Chelemas

Base: Good evening, everyone! I'm Base Goapalakrishna...

Utility: And I'm Utility Beaverhausen!

Base: And you're watching Big Winners and Big Losers! Tonight, we're continuing our segment on everybody's favorite reality TV show, Zombie Death Extreme. Last week, we looked at the big winner of the first season, Zombie Death Extreme-L.A. You know, a lot of people protested when Neeta Lyffe awarded the million dollars to Nasir Haq Qalzai. They thought he was getting a pity win because his country had been invaded by zombies and Iranians. But he proved to be a big winner on and off the show.

Utility: That's right. Rather than selfishly keeping the money or even remaining in the relatively safe United States, he immediately flew back to his homeland to train cadres of exterminators and to fight the undead himself. He's already been awarded two medals of valor, along with Gordon Makepeace, another ZDE competitor who volunteered to help him. Haq Qalzai is a national hero, founder of Afghanistan's first national zombie exterminators guild—and he's finally marrying his childhood sweetheart. Now, that's a winner!

Base: Yep, and today, we're looking at a big winner-turned-big loser! That's right, the surprise sweetheart we all love to hate, Zombie Death Extreme—Bayou winner, Marcel Chelemas.

Utility: Marcel was the drool-worthy early favorite, with that deep Cajun accent, sexy muscles and what we all thought was a solicitous and caring manner. No one was sur-prised when instead of investing his million in an exterminator business, he produced the popular zombie home defense video, You CAN Survive the Zombie Apocalypse. Wow, did he have us fooled.

Base: His true colors started to show at the ZomZeitgeber Convention in San Francisco. He attended ostensibly to sell his videos and do some promotion for the show. As most people who were watching the event know, he was doing some pretty heavy flirting with Neeta Lyffe. Appar-ently, however, flirting was not the only thing on his mind. Check out this clip taken at Neeta's own publicity event after the zombie attack of Richmond.

So this is at the car show, where Neeta was promoting HumVans. She's totally wrecked her knee taking on the zombies the night before. See the look on her face when she sees Chelemas? That's because he attacked her not 24 hours earlier. There's Marcel, trying to talk his way out of trouble by appealing to her boyfriend, can you believe it? That's her sword in Chelemas' hand, by the way. I don't know why he had it. Okay, just listen to this!

Marcel: I told you, yesterday, Ted, we had a misunderstanding, is all. I didn't realize how upset she'd get, or I'd have waited to apologize.

Neeta (voice straining with shock): Misunderstanding? Luring me to your room with the promise of HazMat suits, and then thinking I was going to sleep with you—that would have been a misunderstanding. Tackling me when I refused you—there was nothing unclear about that.

Shouts of outrage, reporters asking questions.

Neeta (voice rising above the chaos): You knocked me to the ground, wrenched my knee, made me miss a Nine-One-One call, and you think that's a misunderstanding?

Marcel: It was play! I was overenthusiastic.

Marcel smiles and shrugs at the reporters as if they'd understand. The glares clearly show they do not sympathize with him.

Neeta: I had to hit you twice to get away. What kind of misunderstanding is that?

Marcel: You are obviously overwrought…

Neeta: You tried to rape me, Marcel Chelemas. I got away. How many didn't?

Neeta activates her monofilament sword. It slices through a soda can. Marcel takes a look at it and runs away.

Utility: For those of you wondering what Neeta means by "luring her in with promise of hazmat suits," remember that just the day before, a huge zombie outbreak had flooded San Francisco and parts of the city of Richmond. All available exterminators were called to duty, and the hazmat suits that protect them from zombie spoor were in short supply. Neeta had already risked her life once taking on the undead on the beach without proper protection. She was looking for a suit, not sex.

Neeta filed charges, but the case never went to court because she managed to escape. Since then, two other women have accused him of sexual assault. Those cases are still in court, so we can't say anything more, except— LOSER!

Base: So personal life: Fail. What about professionally? Well, while Neeta Lyffe was shaking off the attempted assault and then jumping—yes, jumping!—the Broken Bay Bridge in her van to take on the undead swarming a local bar, Chelemas was on the Blabsphere advertising his product. Just listen to his blabs:

LeMarcel: People of SanFran/Richmond. You stay indoors and remember the lessons of my video! I'll keep y'all safe! http:blablink/survivalvid

LeMarcel: Coo! Gonna behead the undead! Y'all stay safe and leave the extermination to me. http:blablink/survivalvid

LeMarcel: It's the zombie apocalypse in SF/Richmond, but you CAN survive. Download my lessons if you want to live! http:blablink/survivalvid

Utility: Oh, no. It's better than that. This was the work of his publicist. Yes, he paid someone to post these tasteless ads during a full-out zombie crisis. He was hanging out in his hotel room until a bellhop had to fetch him. Then, he volunteered to work alongside Neeta's partner, Ted Hacker. How's that for cheek? But he gets his in the end. Here's the raw footage from the Waysterman Refinery. That's the one that makes sewage-based fuels for the GovMo CrapMaster. Keep that in mind as you watch the guy in the front, the one with his hands out. That's Marcel!

The black-and white footage from the cheap security camera showed the inside of the refinery. Pipes leaked steam and a large, bloated tank expanded slowly, the metal bending unnaturally. A security guard—or maybe a zombie—was twisting a valve. Toward the back, an exterminator hacked at a pair of zombies while Marcel stood in the foreground, his hands out as if expecting a package to fall from the heavens. Then, he dropped his arms, hunched a moment, and tossed his hands up as if exasperated.

Behind him the security guard, now definitely identifiable as undead, rose from its work and started toward the exterminator in the background. The unidentified exterminator twisted his head, saw the zombie, and yelled at Marcel.
Marcel activated his sword and sprang into action, swinging wide and strong. He leapt over the pipe, roaring.

The monofilament blade whipped through the zombie in Marcel's signature uppercut, and he let his momentum take him in a half spin.

The blade sliced the distended metal.

A deluge of pressurized, half-digested feces from farms and city sewers found their escape and poured over Marcel.

Utility: Oh, yeah! Marcel stinks in more ways than one! LOSER!

Base: Well, it's probably no surprise that after those two videos went viral, sales of Marcel's home defense program dropped like a zombie's severed head. Marcel is not taking his fall from grace...well, gracefully. In fact, Chelemas is currently in a medium-security Rehabilitation Facility for the Legally Misunderstood while awaiting trial for assault.

Utility: Yep! Chelemas was arrested Jan 7 at the After-Christmas/Pre-Valentine's Day 70 Percent Off Sale at ChangeMart in Belle Adona, Louisiana, for beating 60-

year-old Etsy artist Matilda Flynn with copies of his own zombie survival program. Matilda was loading her cart with Chelemas' videos to use as materials for her next big commercial arts project. Who could blame her, when they were only a dollar?

Base: Oh, yeah, you can't buy the materials for that price. If I made coffee tables out of microdiscs and plastic de-collage, I'd snatch them up, too. Apparently, however, Chelemas just isn't into Reuse—Recycle where his own worthless videos are concerned. The store security tape has been sealed until the trial, but rumor says he threw a celebrity fit to rival that of Transgen Tata when someone called xer a "he."

Utility: Ooo! I won't forget that tantrum anytime soon, and I'm sure our viewers won't either. Now listen, if any of you happened to be at ChangeMart on the day in question and caught Chelemas' little meltdown on your phones, we have a prize for you. Just tap that button on the bottom of your screen to contact us. In the meantime, Marcel wins the Big Winners and Big Losers Prize for Biggest Loser of All. Good night, and may you all be winners!

Global Fattening: Definitive Proof that Humans Aren't Healthy for the Earth

In 2024, President Guildhaus launched the National Temperature Normalization Initiative and directed the NOAA to enforce its regulations for positioning temperature sensing stations, removing them from areas that radiated heat, such as black-topped parking lots and rooftop hot-air vents. She also authorized the replacement of old, overpainted heat-sink cases, replacing them with protective boxes that didn't hold in heat, but rather kept the box's internal temperature the same as the temperature around it. By the time her tenure was over in 2028, the initiative had completed and the mean recorded temperature of the nation had dropped three degrees overall.

The new administration declared a Global Cooling Emergency and created the Global Winter Accountability and Negation Operation (GWA-NO) which conducted a seven-year study that concluded that America's industries and use of artificial chemicals and fossil fuels had caused the problem. Meanwhile, countries around the world had also begun changing their temperature tracking stations. As recorded temperatures decreased, the UN blamed the United States for starting an "environmental pandemic." Some progressive environmentalist defenders, however, saw the mixed logic and sought a more concrete reason to prove humans were destroying the earth.

In 2013, a joint Australian-German research team led by Curtin University's Dr. Christian Hirt created the highest-resolution maps of Earth's gravity field to date—showing gravitational variations up to 40 per cent larger than previously assumed. The study was heralded in the press as mildly interesting before returning to the real crisis of Global Warming. However, in 2030, environmentalists unsatisfied with the Global Cooling theory and its ability to enact legislative changes dusted off and reinterpreted the study and commissioned new satellites. The theory of Global Fattening was born, fed by the Hank Johnson Institute for Global Science and Weight Management. This august organization was named in honor of the Democratic senator who heroically stymied a top military official testifying for the expansion of Guam Air Force Base by demanding to know what steps the Department of Defense would take to prevent the island of Guam from tipping over as a result of the increased population and equipment on the base.

Fueled by environmental activism and the conviction that thin equals healthy, Global Fattening became accepted as the logical consequence to the unnatural increase of manmade materials—both human and technological—and all its poisonous elements. Trending Science has this to say about Global Fattening: *At last, a comprehensive tie between runaway overpopulation and the environment. It's more nefarious than we thought. Never mind drought, crop failure and poverty. We have caused the Earth to change its gravitational integrity!*

Government Motors: A Bold Step in Government-Assisted Capitalism

After the second government bail-out of an American automobile manufacturer in 2025, Congress passed the "You Break It, We Buy It" Act.

From then on, rather than subsidizing dying companies, it simply bought them outright and ran them itself. This move was heralded by the press as the next logical step in compassionate support of American capitalism.

Government Motors was the first success story; after a mere decade of planning, reorganizing and synergizing, it launched its own line of cars: the economy compact, Refund; the luxury SUV, Entitlement; and the muscle car, Poise. Its most recent product line, the CrapMaster pickup, which runs on manure-based fuels, had a setback in the fuel supply when radical environmentalist zombies attacked the experimental manure refinery. Check out the commercial here: https://www.youtube.com/watch?v=op7lup-KFcI

Less successful acquisitions include the California Dust Bowl Solar Farm (CDBSF). "Rescued" by the government in 2032, it made a tidy profit only after the Federal government tapped into public electrical lines and forced California Dust Bowl Energies to buy back the excess electricity produced by the solar farm. In 2035, however, California Dust Bowl Energies (CDBE) declared Chapter 11. It sought government assistance, but

Congress refused, asserting that it would then be competing against itself.

A proposal was raised by Representative Phelin Greene (D-CA) that the rights to CDBSF cede to the Democrats while the Republicans take over the CDBE. However, it was knocked down in a dual-party filibuster that the Washington Post editorial described as the best example of congressional co-operation since it gave itself a 7% raise in 2034. Subsequently, the CDBE closed its doors, and the CDBSF went dark a few months later. On a positive note, Survival Hardware, Inc. saw record sales that year as residents of the Dust Bowl area invested in independent generators.

Dear Zoe Explains LAID Therapy

Dear Zoe, a popular manners and advice blogger of the 2030s, wrote a best-selling book, *How to Tell Your Best Friend You Saw Her Mother Making Out with an Older Woman and Other Awkward Conversations.* Chapter Seventeen dealt with meeting unknown siblings from one-night stands. It's too bad Mandy's mother never bought a copy of that book. She might have had a more congenial meeting with Neeta's mother. Here's just one of Dear Zoe's many popular blog posts concerning affairs—or alternative sexual activities—among veterans.

Dear Zoe, My man has taken up with hoes! Once a month—once a month!—he and a buddy go to the ho factory and get it on with gods-know what. And then he has the nerve to tell me he has to do it on account of losing his legs in the war. He actually said, "My doctor told me if I didn't get laid, I'd go crazy."

I am hurt and I am furious. I drove down there ready to torch the place, but it's connected to the hospital! WTF?

Zoe, you'd better talk me down before I get the gasoline and Styrofoam pellets, anyways!

        - Ain't Gonna Let No Ho Do My Man

Dear "Ain't Gonna,"

Oh, you poor sweet thing! I completely understand your confusion. Obviously, you and your boyfriend have some communication issues to work through, but hopefully, I can help you better understand what's going on.

First of all, I want you to recognize that this is not your fault. Just say that to yourself: It's not my fault. Release that self-blame into the wild.

There. Better? Now you are open to understanding, which is my job to assist you with.

LAID—or Love and Acceptance Insertion for the Disabled—is a relatively new therapy. (I know! Terrible name. You should never refer to the alternately limbed as "disabled.") Started by our progressive neighbors to the north, those forward-thinking Canadians, it involves connecting the mobility challenged with one or more willing strangers for impersonal sexual encounters. The purpose, of course, is to reassure those courageous individuals that even though they may not have full control (terrible word, I know, but this is medicine!)—full control of their limbs that they still have it going on…as one compelling author so charmingly put it…"down there."

You see, "Ain't Gonna"? Your male-identifying partner is being completely honest with you. It is therapy! Your masculine-inclined romantic interest is completely correct, and I applaud him and his doctor for taking these brave, difficult steps in ensuring his mental health. I hope now, you can, too.

Now, don't be worried about the people he may encounter in these vital therapeutic sessions. They are, in fact, volunteers who generously give of their time and talent to help raise the self-esteem of those whom life so cruelly enabled differently. They are regularly screened for STDs by Planned Parenthood and receive extensive training in everything from technique to pillow talk, sometimes at the hands of the therapists themselves. In fact, if you truly care for your romantic comrade—and I'd guess you do since you were willing to burn down a hospital for him!—then you might want to consider volunteering yourself. It would be a beautiful testimony to how you respect your relationship and support his efforts to secure his mental health.

I'm so sorry your gender-specified boyfriend wasn't fully forthcoming about his therapy. Perhaps there's a communication issue stemming from his injuries, or he's simply embarrassed. It's not easy for the testosterone-inclined to admit to having a deep-seated emotional void that only casual hook-ups can fill. So, put the gasoline in the car's tank, and perhaps you and he could find a more creative use for all those Styrofoam pellets together. ☺😺

Oh, my Heck! BYU vs. University of Utah

Narrator: This week on Lingo Across America, we're traveling north and west to the state of Utah. Utah has some distinctive pronunciations, from the dropping of the T when followed by an –en sound, such as in "Lay-en" to the unusual pronunciations of its city names.

Today, however, we have two linguistic sociologists to examine that uniquely Utahan phrase, "Oh, my heck." The profanity-alternative sprung up in the mid-80s and spread like heck throughout the state, even to the point of becoming the unofficial state motto. In 2030, Utah approved the "Oh, my heck!" license plate, and the phrase achieved nationwide popularity in the 2036 sitcom, *That's My Wife, Too.*

Yet no one knows how this mysterious yet catchy phrase originated. It's my pleasure to welcome Brigham Gonzales of BYU and Truxton Smith of the University of Utah. Gentlemen, what the heck is up with "Oh, my heck?" I mean, why my heck in particular?

Brigham of BYU: An intriguing question of great relevance to the Mormon mind, thank you for asking. Although a modern phrase, it springs from the very teachings of Joseph Smith himself. Joseph Smith taught that faithful Mormons have the potential to become as gods themselves, and of course, as gods, we will be responsible for our own heaven and...well...hell. Therefore, what we're seeing here is an attempt to connect with our inner goodness and a reflection of our Mormon yearning to assume such grand responsibility...

Truxton of U of U: Seriously? How much money did you misappropriate to create such a steaming pile?

Brigham of BYU: Ah, the Ute contributes his opinion—and in the tongue of his people, too. Perhaps you have an alternate origin theory, professor?

Truxton of U of U: What origin theory? We wanted to swear, and we didn't want to get into trouble. If I said, "My God," I'd have gotten my mouth washed out.

Brigham of BYU: So your theory is fear of soap? I can see that would be popular among your students.

Truxton of U of U: Listen, you pompous blowhard. It's bowdlerization, pure and simple. There's no theological underpinnings, no deep philosophy. Some kid who thought it up to keep from getting grounded, and it stuck. It's that way with a lot of language.

Brigham of BYU: I see. You've obviously given this a lot of thought…about on par with that your football coach gives to his plays. As long as we're on the topic of shallow thinking, I'd like to point out that *That's My Wife, Too* was about an agnostic polygamist family. The whole premise was that they didn't know if they believed in marriage. Yet the media has misappropriated the culture and assigned it to Mormonism, when polygamy has never been a Mormon practice.

Truxton of U of U: Right. Just like we never banned coffee. Why are you listening to this guy? He thinks Polygamy is just a fun beer name. Misappropriation of culture? His name's not even Brigham. It's LaHurl. He changed his name so he'd fit better in the culture. It was that or go teach at Weber.

Brigham of BYU: Oh, for pity's… If I pay you for the pizza, will you just go?

Truxton of U of U: Oh, my heck! You did not just use that old line? Go teach your sophomores how to change a lightbulb, will you?

Brigham of BYU: I have to when they transfer from U of U.

Truxton of U of U: You're just bitter your students date all the eligible campus women your age. They like cougars, after all. You'll die a cheesy old man.

Brigham of BYU: What?

Truxton of U of U: *Provo*lone!

Narrator: Okay! Join us tomorrow when we discuss why Utahan's pronounce "Hooper" as "Hupper" and "Mantua" as "Manaway." Oh, my heck! Guys!

About Operation Homefront

Operation Homefront is a legitimate, existing charity that helps service members and wounded warriors with financial help, food assistance, and auto and home repairs. They can assist with relocation moves and provide furniture and other household items to military families in need.

It has created multiple programs for supporting injured military, including the Operation Homefront Village where wounded veterans and their families can find transitional housing where they can live rent-free until the veteran and his family are able to become self-sufficient again. The Hearts of Valor program helps those who care for wounded veterans with retreats, support groups and online forums where others who are helping a spouse who was severely wounded in the war get back on his or her feet—literally and figuratively. In addition, this organization has fundraisers to help provide everything from home loans to school supplies, all geared toward helping the military member and his or her family make the transition to civilian life.

This non-profit has been recognized by several independent charity watchdog organizations for excellent performance. It puts 92 percent of its earnings back into programs to help the military veteran. There are many ways you can help, from donating to giving of your time or talent to one of their many programs. Learn more at http://www.operationhomefront.org.

Thanks for Reading

Did you miss the first two books? Find the Neeta Lyffe series on Amazon.

Publishing this story is a bittersweet experience for me. Barring some unexpected change in fortune, this will be the last Neeta Lyffe, Zombie Exterminator novel.

I started this series back in 2012 with a short story, "Wokking Dead" which appeared in The Zombie Cookbook by Damnation Books. It was really meant to be a lot of zombie slapstick and puns, but people loved Neeta and Ted and asked the publisher for a novel. I was only too happy to oblige. We were stationed in California at the time and the kids were watching Total Drama Island, so the idea of a harried exterminator unwillingly doing reality TV in a world where liberal politics had gone mad was easy and appealing to me.

But that was almost a decade ago. The 2040s, which seemed like a far enough future to write in, are now around the corner. Some of the jokes have not aged well. They've been the subject of bad covers, arguments with Amazon, lost royalties on the audiobooks, and other problems. Meanwhile Vern and the HMB Impulsive want more of my time, as does Gapman, whose story has not been written yet.

So it's time for Neeta and Ted to get their happily ever after. Thank you, dear readers, for loving Neeta as much as I do.

Keep in Touch

If you want to learn about future books, please

- Sign up for my newsletter. https://fabianspace.substack.com/subscribe for extra Vern stories, updates and a free book!

- Visit my website
  (https://karinafabian.com)
- Follow me on Facebook:
  https://www.facebook.com/Karina-Fabian-Speculative-Fiction-with-a-Grin-2233839790277963
- Follow *Vern* on Facebook:
  https://www.facebook.com/DragonEyePI
- Join HuFleet—follow the Impulsive on Facebook:

  https://www.facebook.com/sthmb/

Acknowledgements

Shambling in a Winter Wonderland has had a long history of fits and starts. I started it as a fundraiser for Operation Homefront when my husband was deployed, but unlike my other serial stories, it didn't garner steady donations. Even more, my heart wasn't in it at the time, so when the second week went by without anyone tossing in a dollar or two to keep it moving, I succumbed to the inevitable and let it drop off.

Even though the story sat for a couple of years, it still played out in my mind, so in 2014, I decided to finish it. My friend and editor, Jamie Wilson, provided coaching and inspired me to really work on the serial aspect. It had a brief run in Liberty Island in early 2015 before I decided to novelize it. Even though the novel is no longer a serial, the flow is there because it worked so well in the novel as well. Thanks for the coaching, Jamie!

As part of the novelization, I wanted to add some of the asides and social/cultural/political silliness that I loved about Neeta Lyffe, Zombie Exterminator. Thus, I'd like to thank my friends at Top Ten Reviews/Purch (my day job when I first started writing this) for all their help: Kent Dunn for assistance with the BYU/U of U rivalry; Jeph Preece for sharing his surfing experience, and Beth Johnson, Mike McPeek, Ben Davis, and Alisha Clark for the discussion on language. John Konecsni (aka Declan Finn) shared a particularly ridiculous article on FB that give me the most wondrously wicked idea for LAID therapy. My son Liam accidentally put whipped cream instead of whipped butter in a roll at a buffet and sparked the idea of High Snackage, which Becca Butcher helped me develop.

After letting the story sit for too many years while I tried to get the series rebooted, I read over the manuscript and felt like some of the asides interrupted the flow rather than enhanced the story. I hated to lose them, so you'll find them in the Bonus Content. (Thanks go to Jane Lebak for the suggestion.)

Of course, if anything is inaccurate, I either got it wrong by accident or I did it on purpose. Either way, blame or credit me as you will.

No good story goes straight from the author's head to the publisher's desk—at least not in my case. Thanks to the beta readers of my novel for their feedback: Jill Bowers Carter, Marina Fontaine, Melanie Hamilton, and Joseph Goodwin. Michelle Buckman, who is one of the best writers I know, critiqued a couple of key scenes. This is especially noteworthy as she is neither a big zombie fan or a big SFF fan. That's friendship! Natalie Bagby proofed the version you are holding today. Thanks, Natalie!

As always, thanks to my husband for his support and having the perfect word at the perfect time. (In this case, "bowdlerization," the replacement of something offensive (such as swear words) with something inoffensive.)

There's More Fun in FabianSpace!

Thank you for buying this book. If you enjoyed it, click to see the others in this series or discover one of the other worlds of FabianSpace.

Science Fiction

Space Traipse: Hold My Beer: Redneck ingenuity and common sense in a Star Trek-ish universe. Enjoy the adventures of the *HMB Impulsive*.

The Rescue Sisters: Intrepid women doing dangerous missions in space for the love of God and humankind.

The Old Man and the Void: Dex is a relic hunter on the edge of the black hole, desperate for the catch of a lifetime.

Jovian Heat: As the next Great Storm of Jupiter rises, Cass must find the father of a baby in peril—but the father died before the child was conceived.

Fantasy

DragonEye Story: Vern's a snarky dragon on the wrong side of the Interdimensional Gap, solving crimes, battling evil, and saving the universes on an all-too-regular basis.

Madness of Kanaan: Deryl isn't crazy; he's psychic, and aliens of two worlds thinks he can save them. Maybe he can—but can he regain his sanity in the process?

Horror

Neeta Lyffe, Zombie Exterminator: Neeta's an average exterminator, taking out bugs, rodents, and the undead. Can she keep her friends alive, pay her bills, and find romance?

Frightliner and Other Tales of the Supernatural (with Colleen Drippé): Truck-driving vampires terrorizing the road, Southern women doing what needs doing, a zombie wedding—a great story collection for horror lovers.

ABOUT THE AUTHOR

Karina Fabian is easily freaked out by horror films and Stephen King novels but does enjoy comedy horror. She enjoys comedy in just about anything, and it shows in her writing. She married a rocket scientist who is now COO of Vaya Space. They live in their dream home which has been pimped out in Geek Chic. She has four adult children, two dogs, and more stories in her head than she can get out in one lifetime. But she's trying!